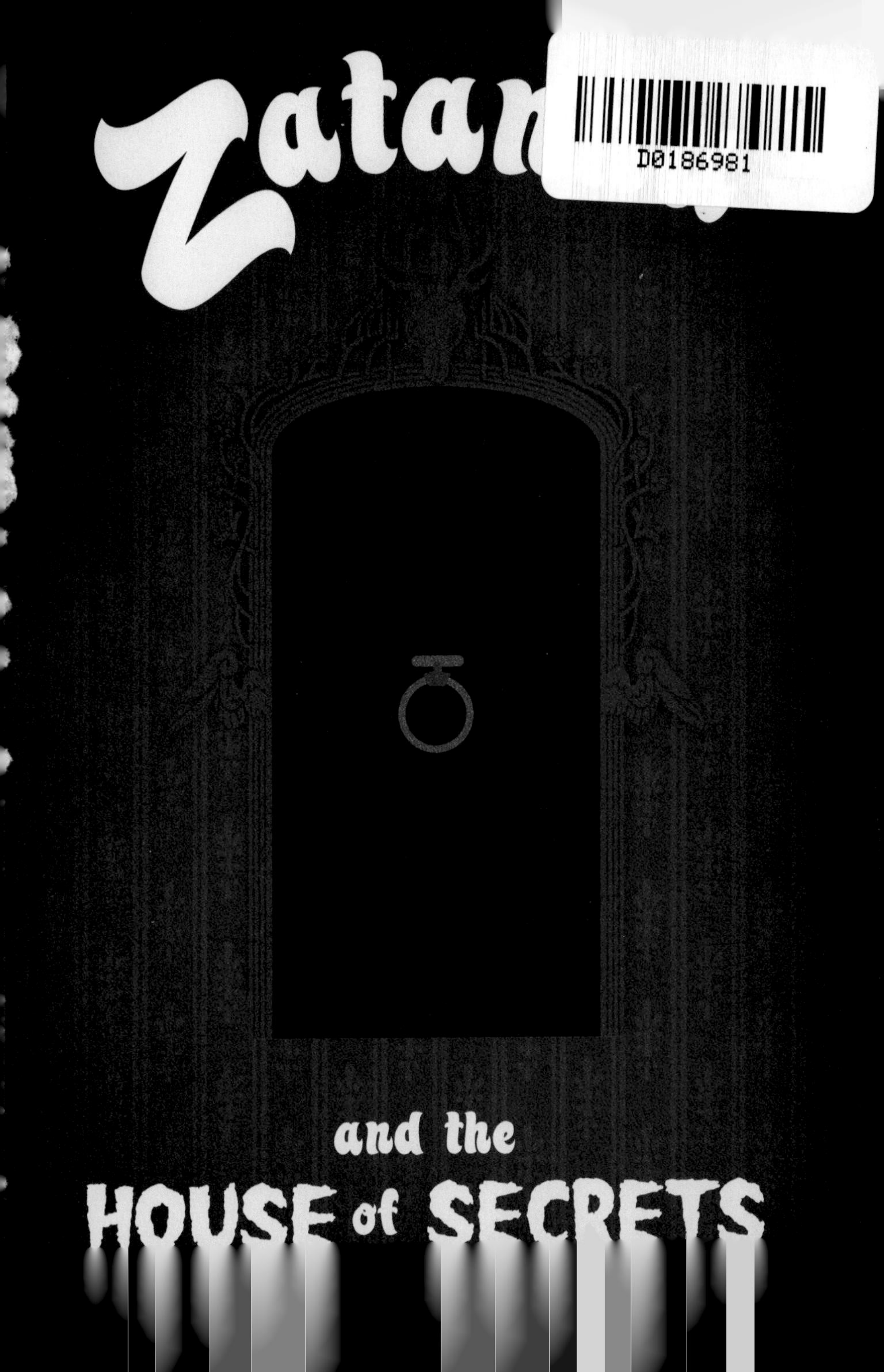
Zatan
and the
HOUSE of SECRETS

Matthew Cody

AUTHOR

Yoshi Yoshitani

ARTIST

Ariana Maher

LETTERER

Zatanna

and the
HOUSE of SECRETS

Zatanna created by Gardner Fox and Murphy Anderson

ALEX R. CARR Editor
DIEGO LOPEZ Associate Editor
STEVE COOK Design Director - Books
AMIE BROCKWAY-METCALF Publication Design

BOB HARRAS Senior VP - Editor-in-Chief, DC Comics
MICHELE R. WELLS VP & Executive Editor, Young Reader

DAN DiDIO Publisher
JIM LEE Publisher & Chief Creative Officer
BOBBIE CHASE VP - New Publishing Initiatives &
Talent Development
DON FALLETTI VP - Manufacturing Operations &
Workflow Management
LAWRENCE GANEM VP - Talent Services
ALISON GILL Senior VP - Manufacturing & Operations
HANK KANALZ Senior VP - Publishing Strategy & Support Services
DAN MIRON VP - Publishing Operations
NICK J. NAPOLITANO VP - Manufacturing Administration & Design
NANCY SPEARS VP - Sales

ZATANNA AND THE HOUSE OF SECRETS

DC Comics, 2900 West Alameda Ave.,
Burbank, CA 91505
Printed by LSC Communications, Crawfordsville,
IN, USA. 1/10/20. First Printing.
ISBN: 978-1-4012-9070-2

Library of Congress Cataloging-in-Publication Data

Names: Cody, Matthew, writer. | Yoshitani, Yoshi, artist. | Maher, Ariana,
    letterer.
Title: Zatanna and the house of secrets : a graphic novel / writer, Matthew
    Cody ; artist, Yoshi Yoshitani ; letterer, Ariana Maher.
Description: Burbank, CA : DC Comics, [2020] | Audience: Ages 8-12 |
    Audience: Grades 4-6 | Summary: Zatanna and her professional magician
    father live in a house full of magic, puzzles, and storybook creatures,
    but when she stands up to a bully in school, she returns home to find
    her father's gone missing within their own home.
Identifiers: LCCN 2019042101 (print) | LCCN 2019042102 (ebook) | ISBN
    9781401290702 (paperback) | ISBN 9781779502049 (ebook)
Subjects: LCSH: Graphic novels. | CYAC: Graphic novels. | Magic—Fiction. |
    Fathers and daughters—Fiction. | Mystery and detective stories.
Classification: LCC PZ7.7.C626 Zat 2020 (print) | LCC PZ7.7.C626 (ebook)
    | DDC 741.5/973—dc23

PEFC Certified

This product is from
sustainably managed
forests and controlled
sources

PEFC
PEFC/29-31-337   www.pefc.org

TABLE of CONTENTS

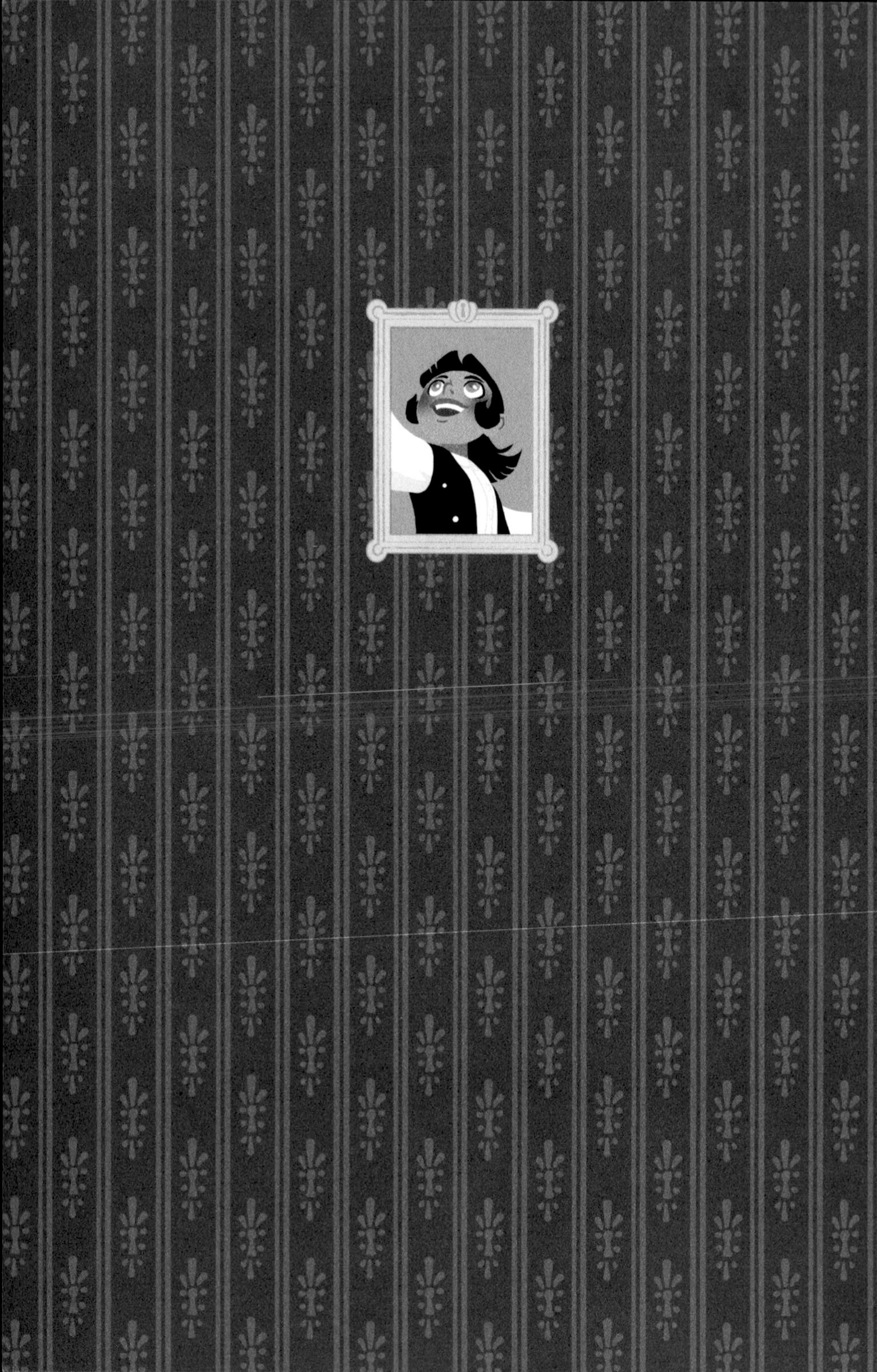

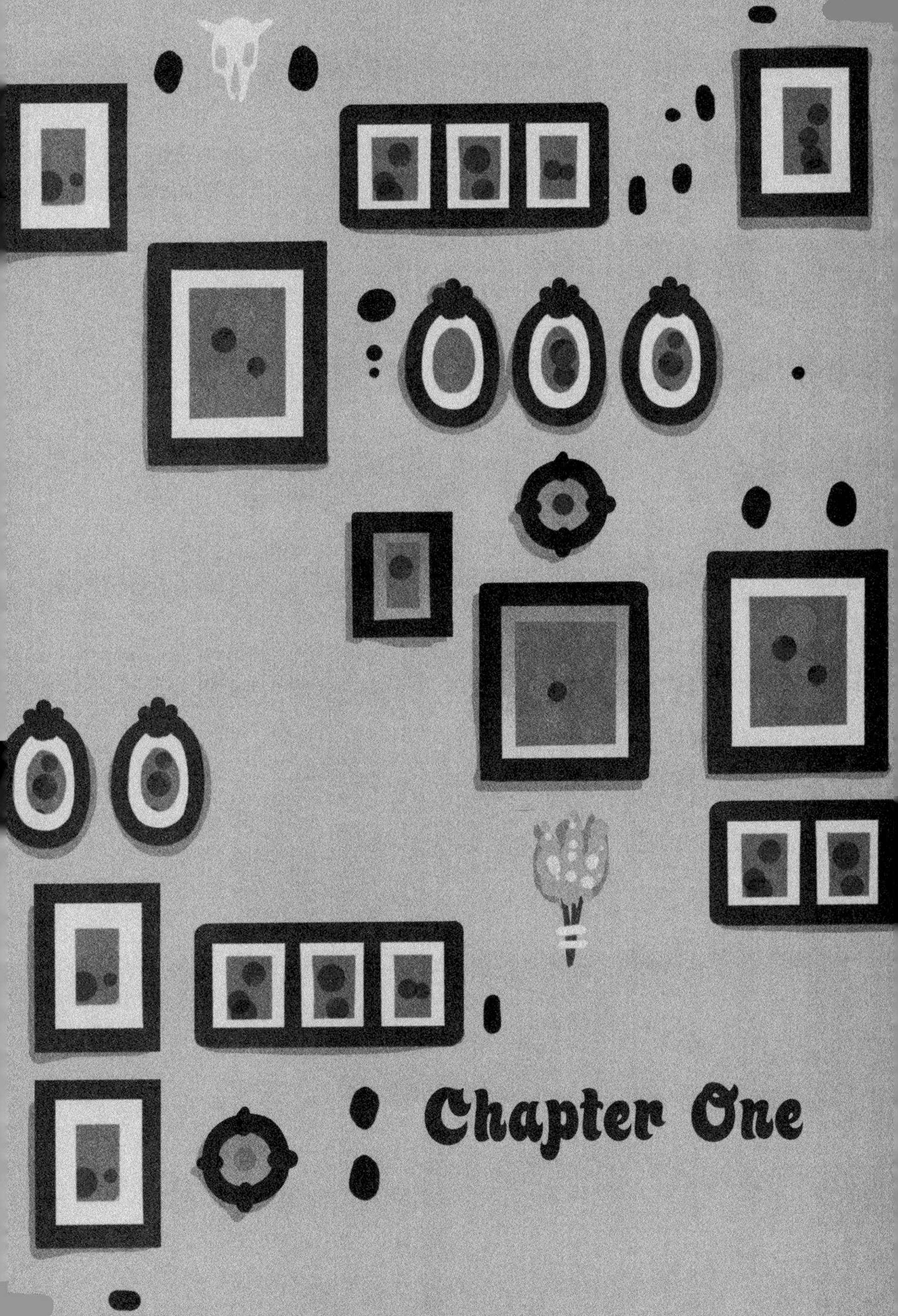

Chapter One

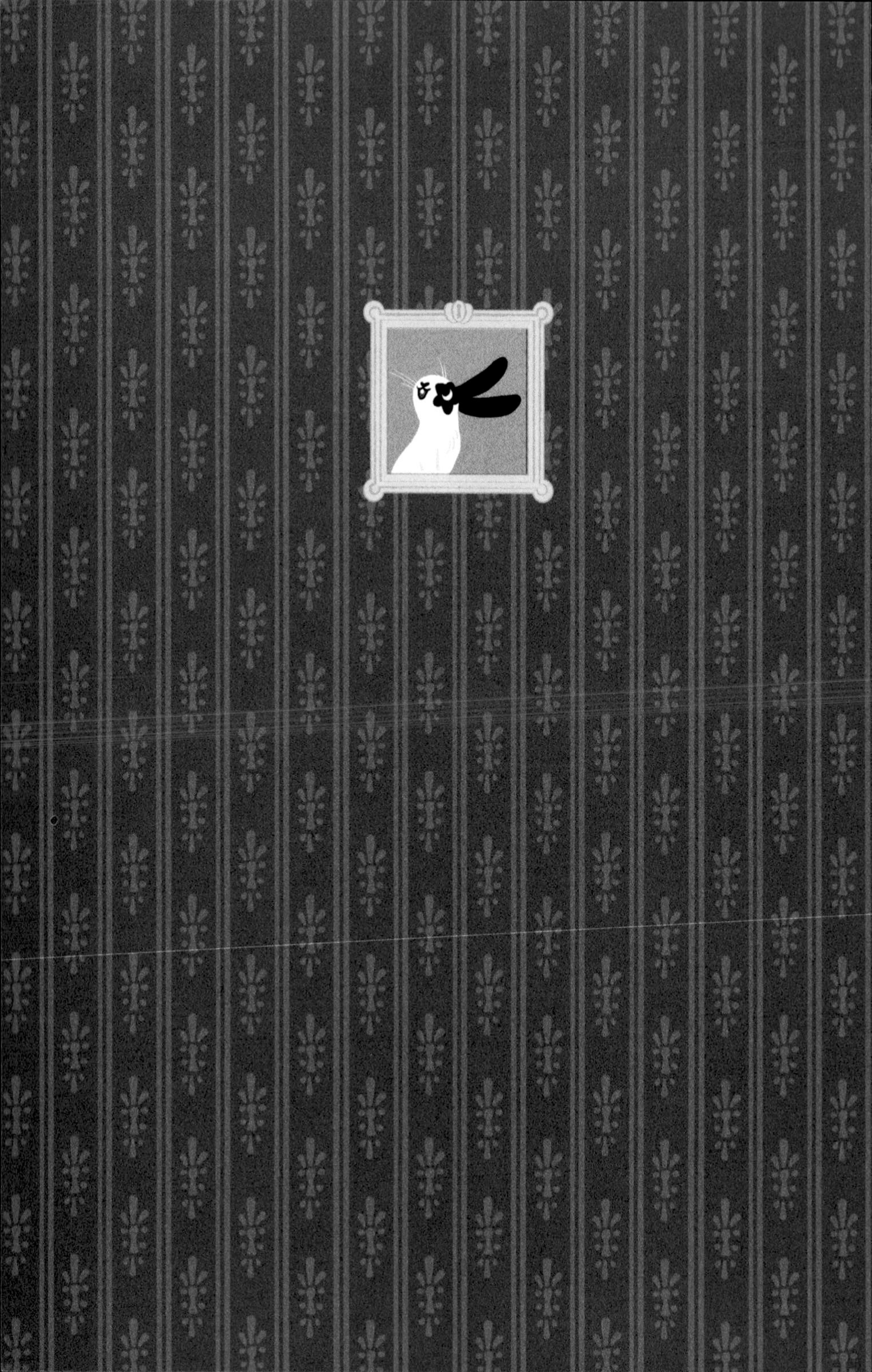

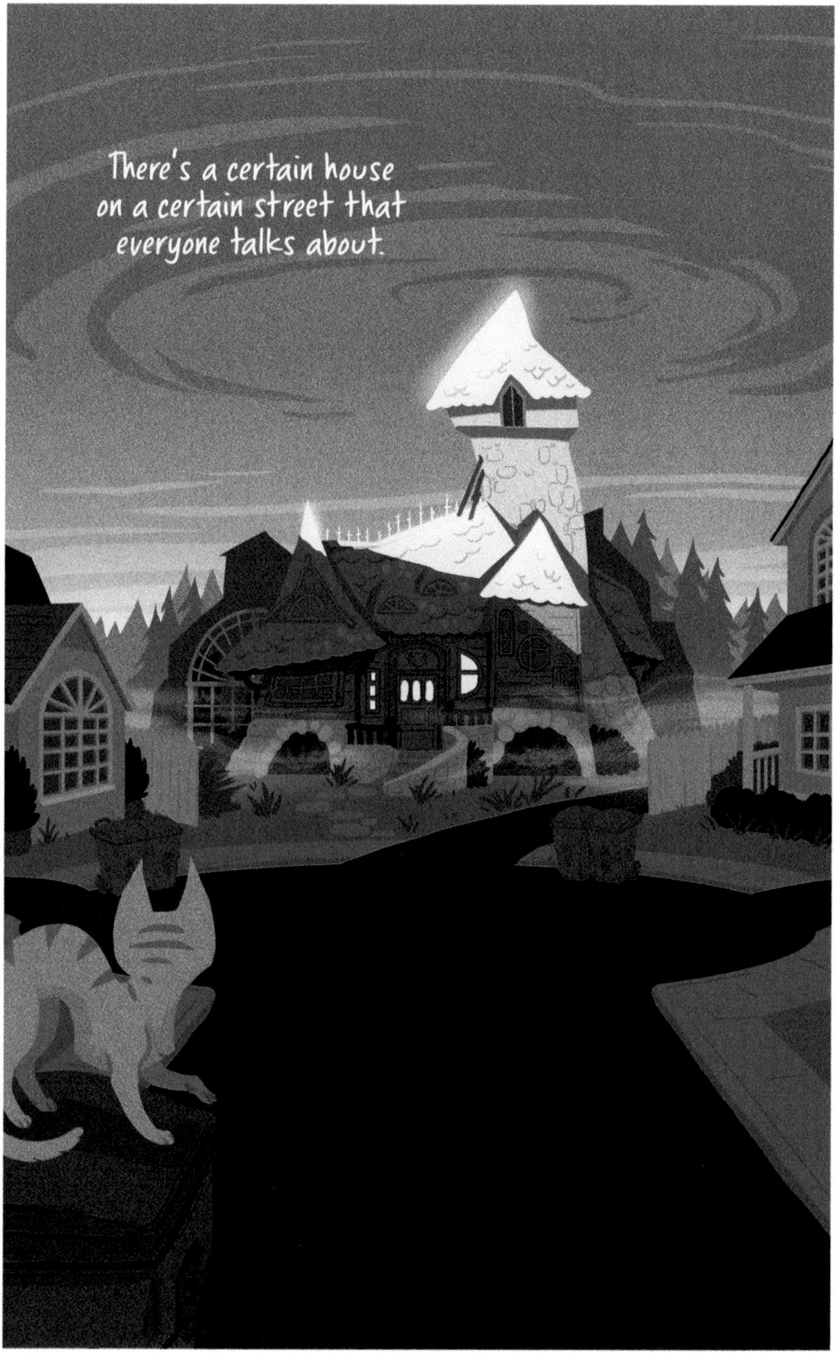
There's a certain house on a certain street that everyone talks about.

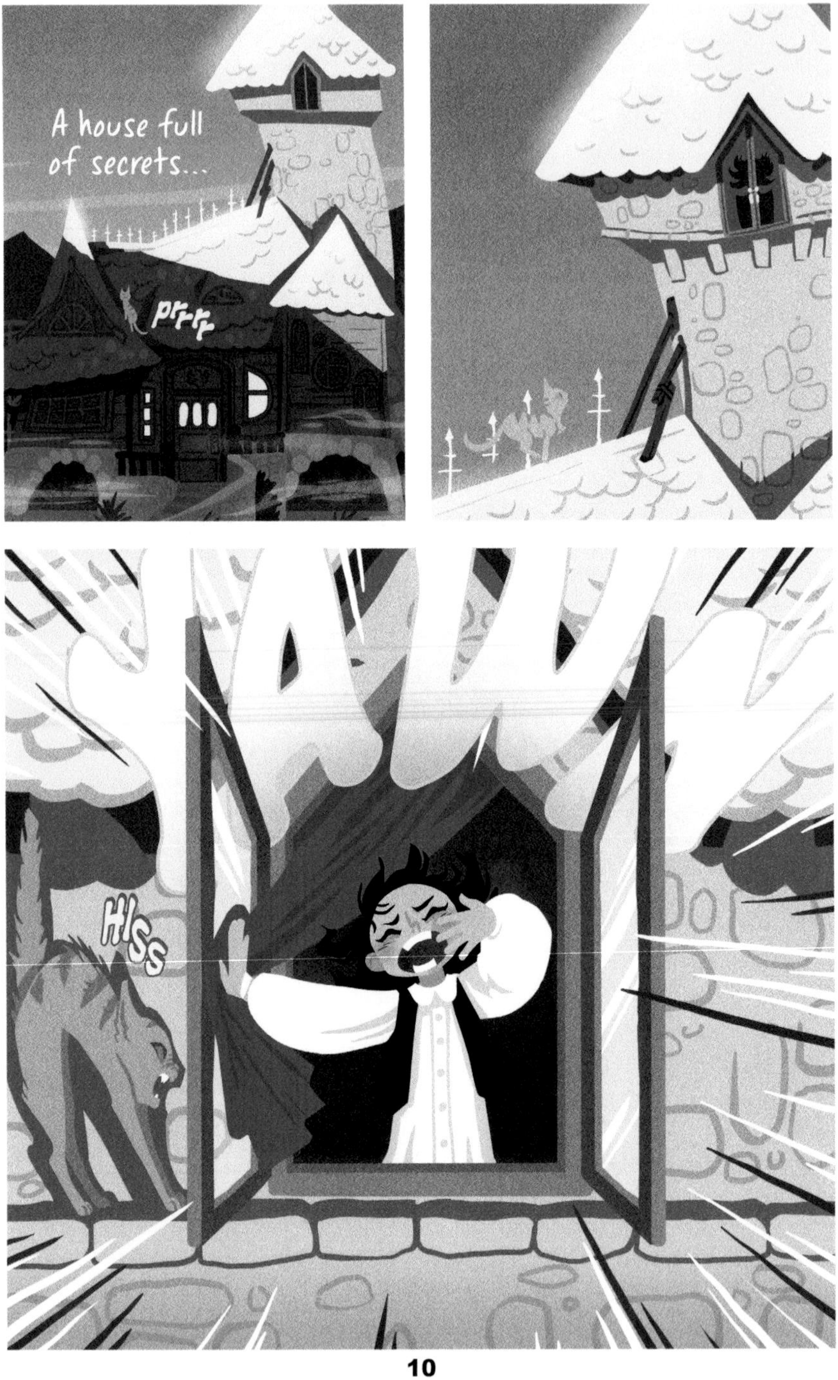
A house full of secrets...
prrrr
HISS

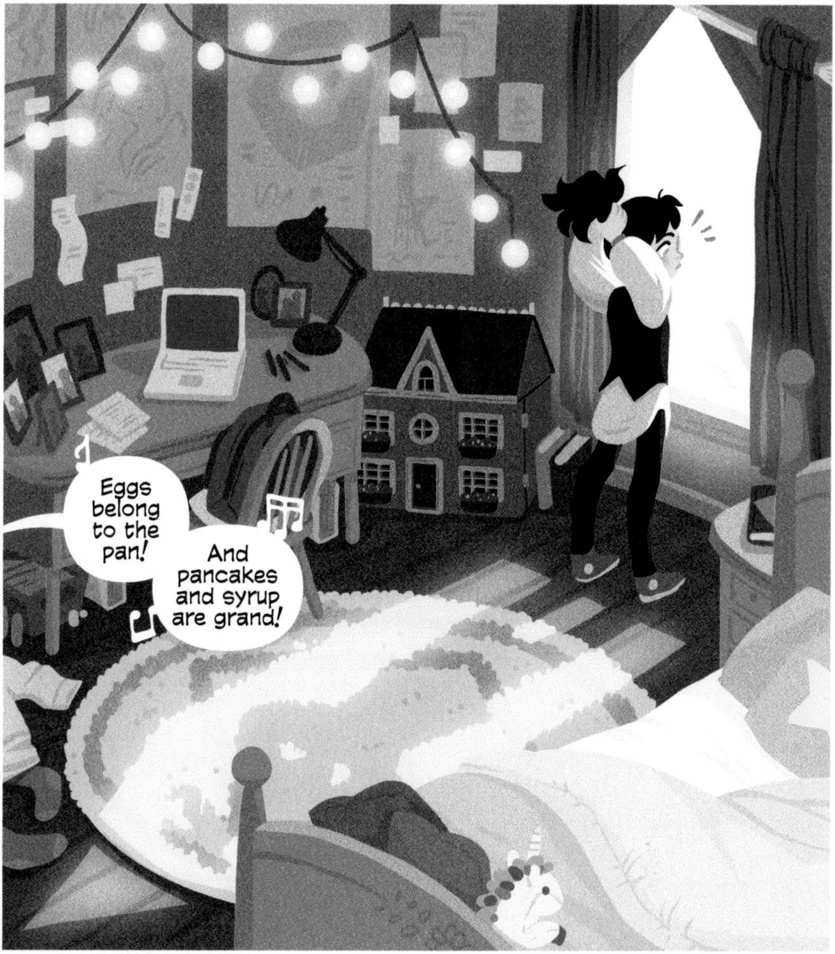
Eggs belong to the pan!
And pancakes and syrup are grand!

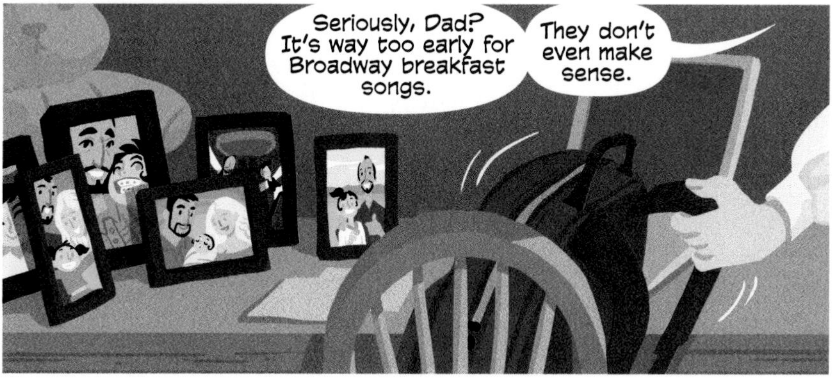
Seriously, Dad? It's way too early for Broadway breakfast songs.
They don't even make sense.

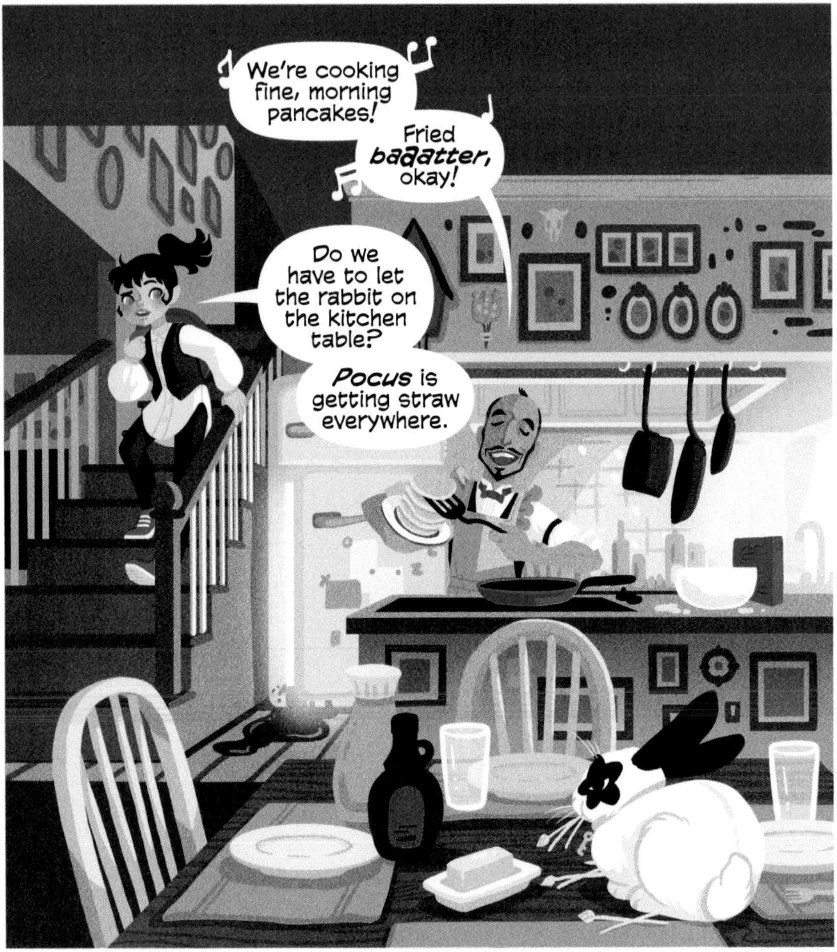
We're cooking fine, morning pancakes!
Fried *baaatter,* okay!
Do we have to let the rabbit on the kitchen table?
Pocus is getting straw everywhere.

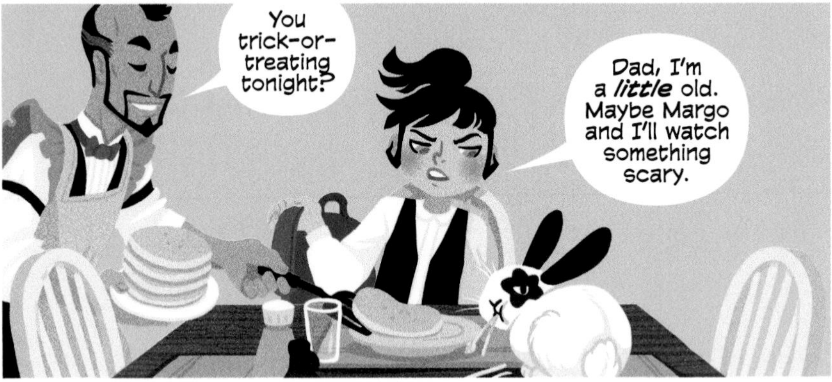
You trick-or-treating tonight?
Dad, I'm a *little* old. Maybe Margo and I'll watch something scary.

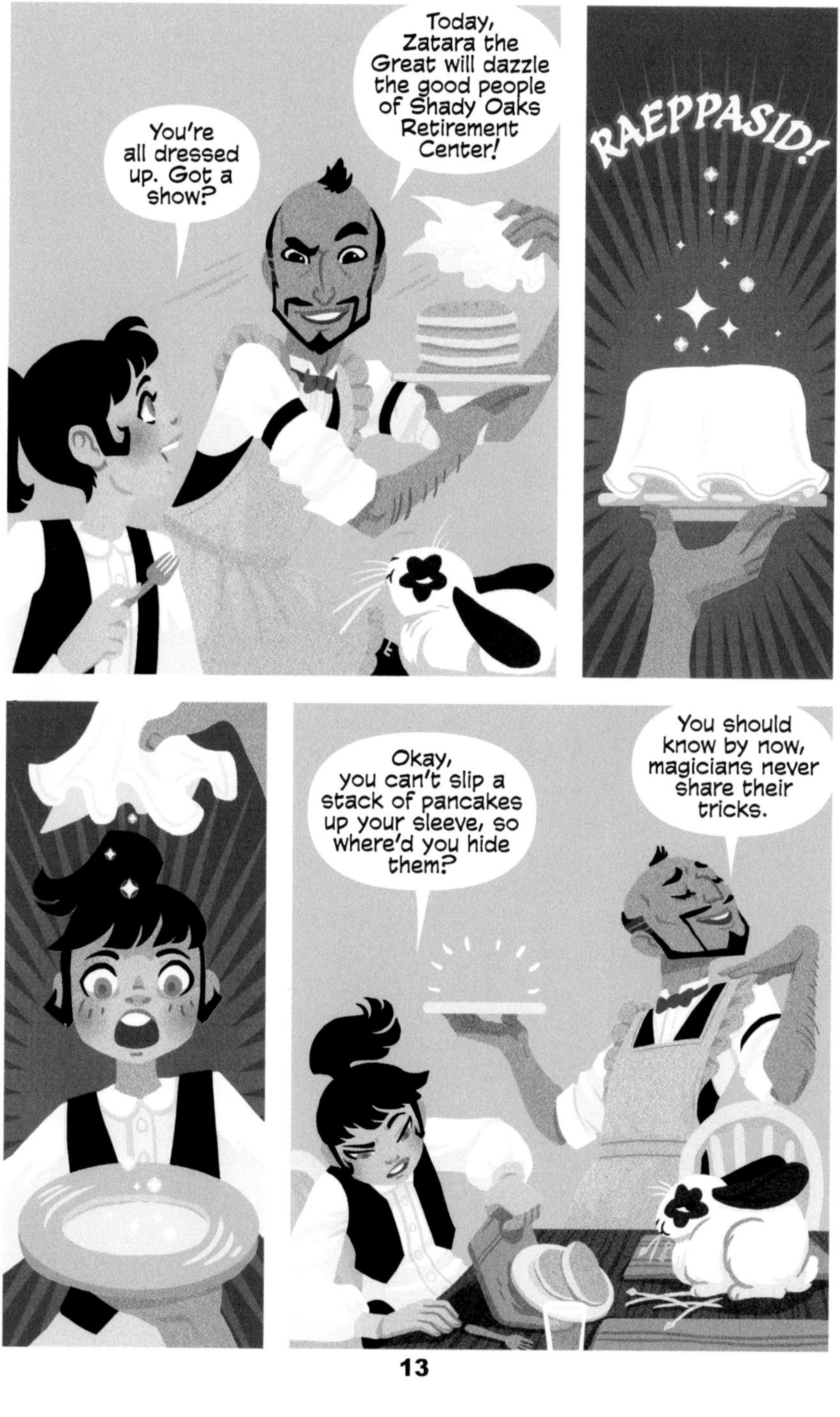
You're all dressed up. Got a show?
Today, Zatara the Great will dazzle the good people of Shady Oaks Retirement Center!
RAEPPASID!
Okay, you can't slip a stack of pancakes up your sleeve, so where'd you hide them?
You should know by now, magicians never share their tricks.

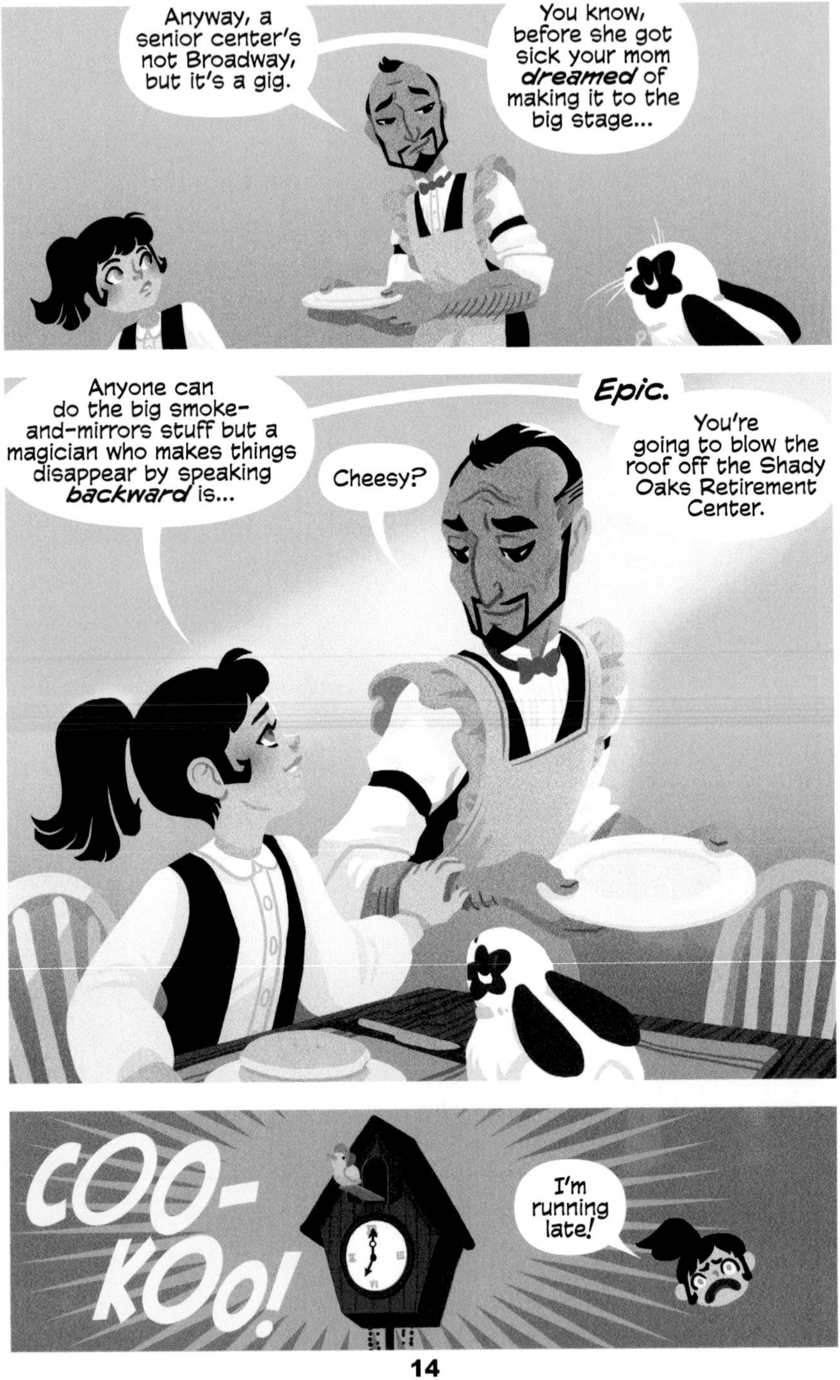
Anyway, a senior center's not Broadway, but it's a gig.
You know, before she got sick your mom *dreamed* of making it to the big stage...
Anyone can do the big smoke-and-mirrors stuff but a magician who makes things disappear by speaking *backward* is...
Cheesy?
Epic.
You're going to blow the roof off the Shady Oaks Retirement Center.
COO-KOO!
I'm running late!

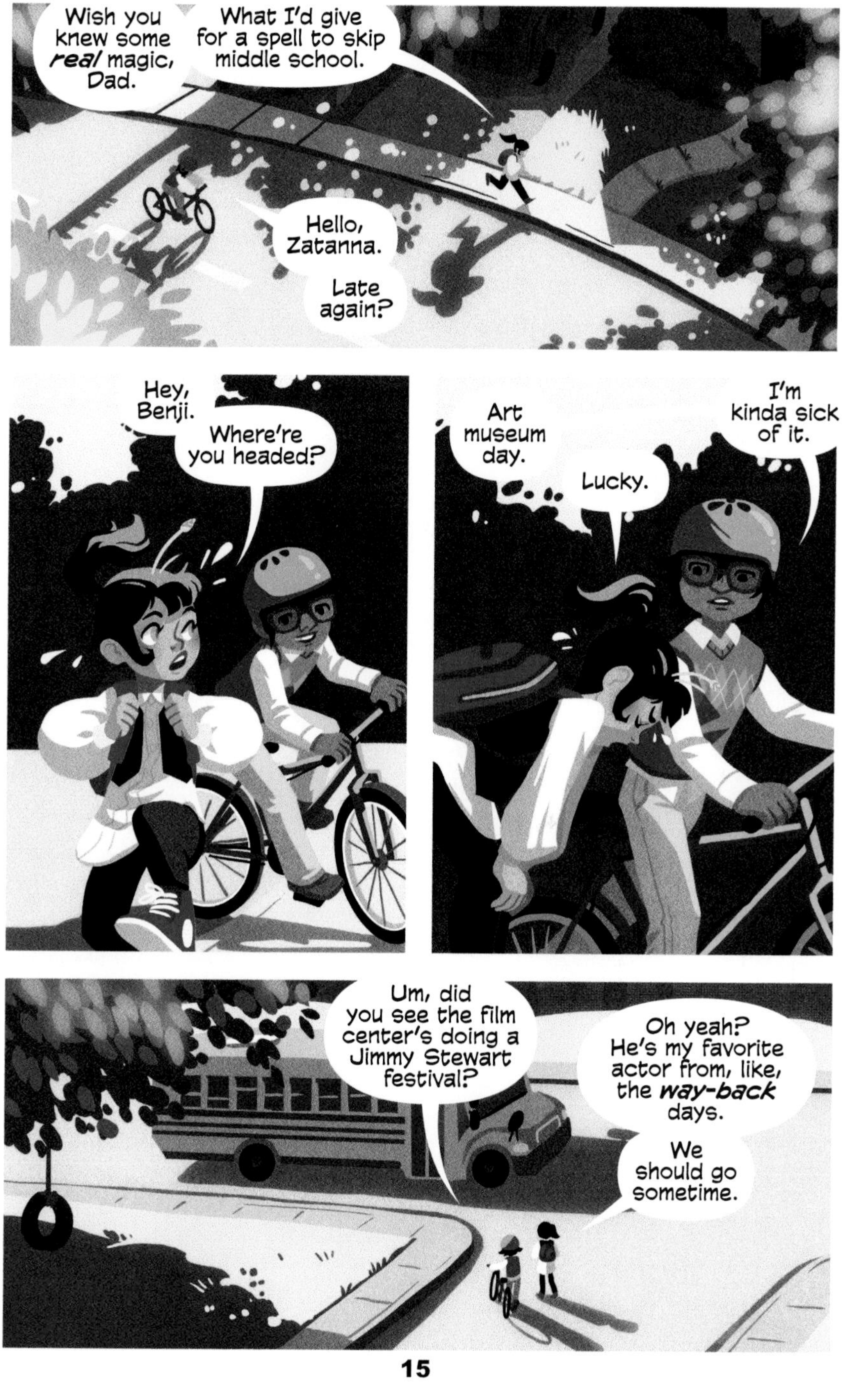
Wish you knew some *real* magic, Dad.
What I'd give for a spell to skip middle school.
Hello, Zatanna.
Late again?
Hey, Benji.
Where're you headed?
Art museum day.
Lucky.
I'm kinda sick of it.
Um, did you see the film center's doing a Jimmy Stewart festival?
Oh yeah? He's my favorite actor from, like, the *way-back* days.
We should go sometime.

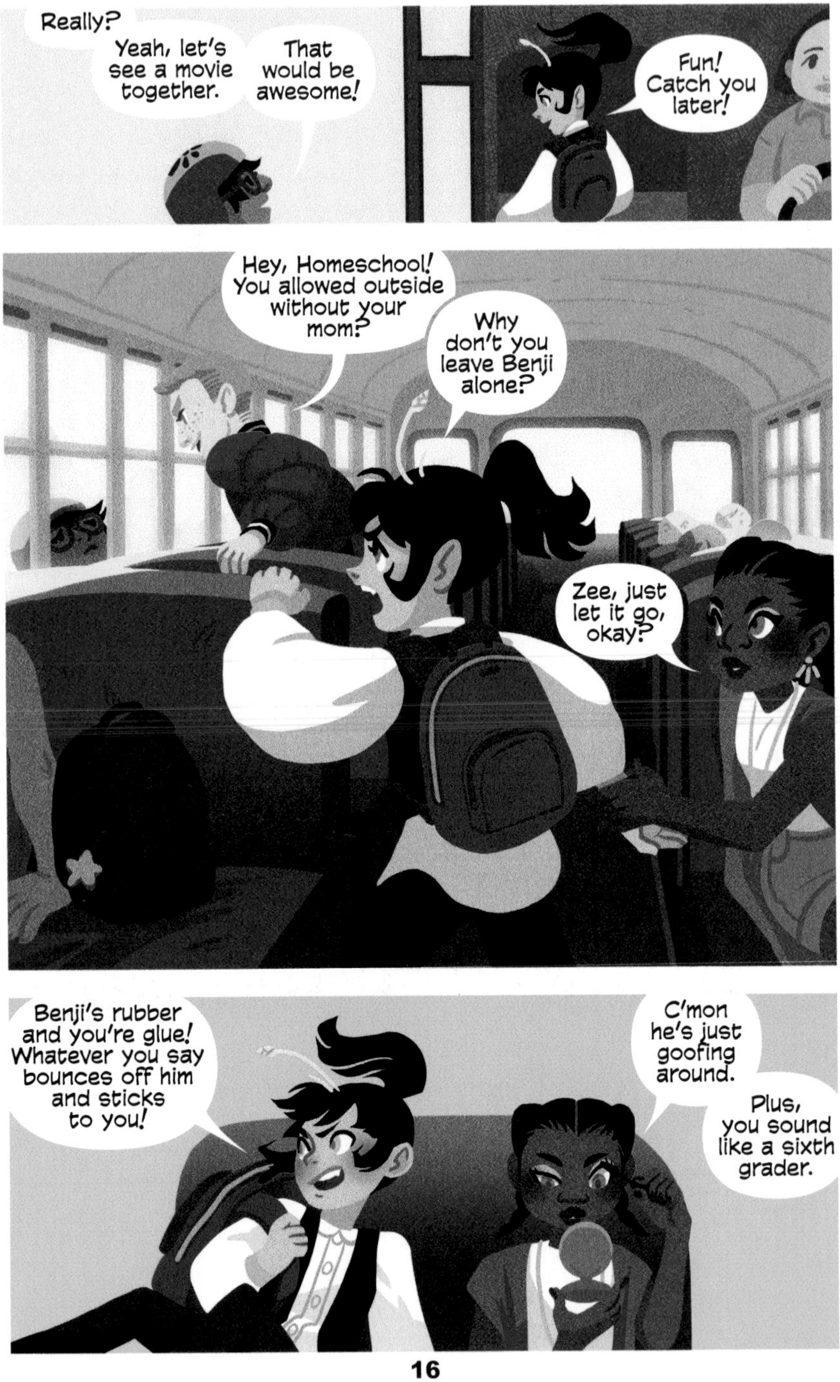
Really?
Yeah, let's see a movie together.
That would be awesome!
Fun! Catch you later!
Hey, Homeschool! You allowed outside without your mom?
Why don't you leave Benji alone?
Zee, just let it go, okay?
Benji's rubber and you're glue! Whatever you say bounces off him and sticks to you!
C'mon he's just goofing around.
Plus, you sound like a sixth grader.

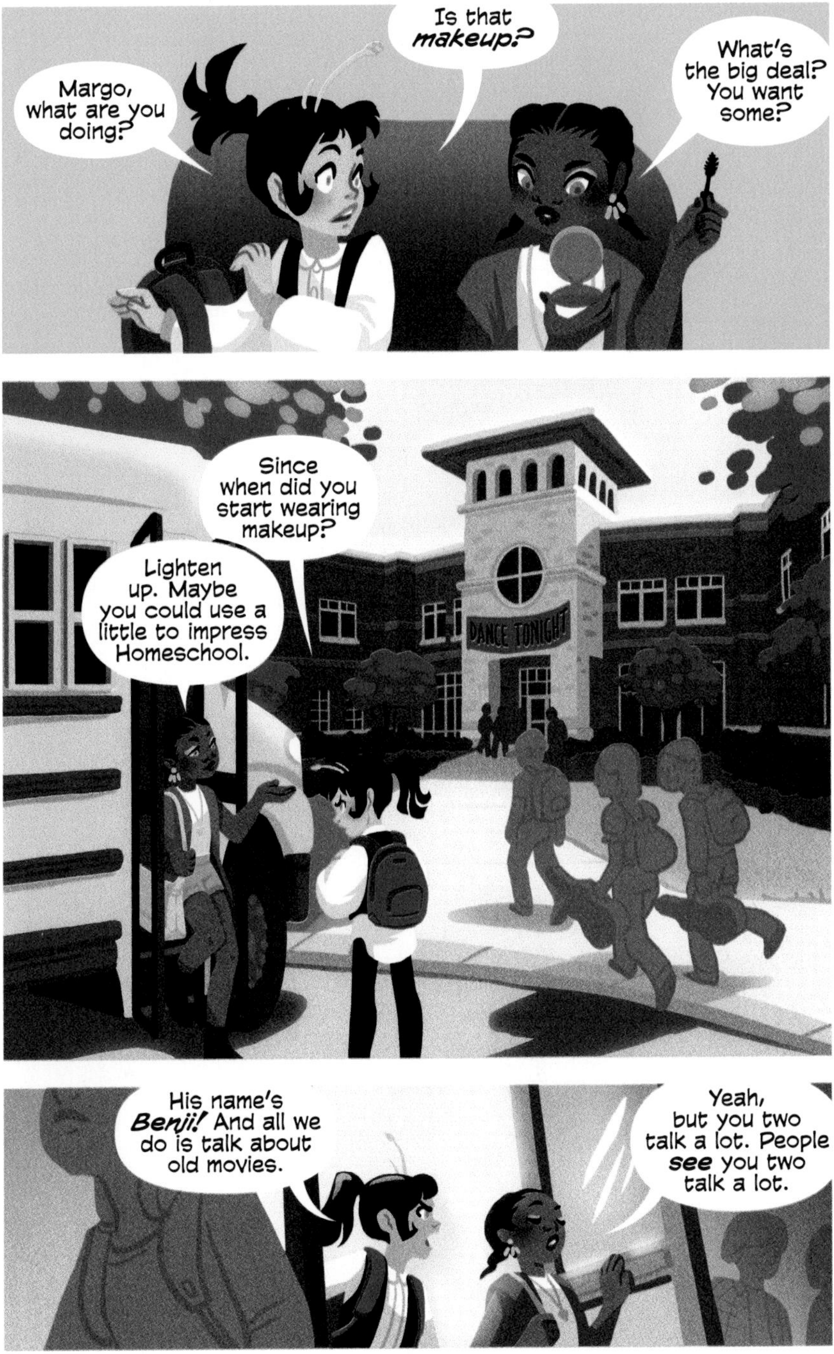
Margo, what are you doing?
Is that *makeup?*
What's the big deal? You want some?
Since when did you start wearing makeup?
Lighten up. Maybe you could use a little to impress Homeschool.
DANCE TONIGHT
His name's *Benji!* And all we do is talk about old movies.
Yeah, but you two talk a lot. People *see* you two talk a lot.

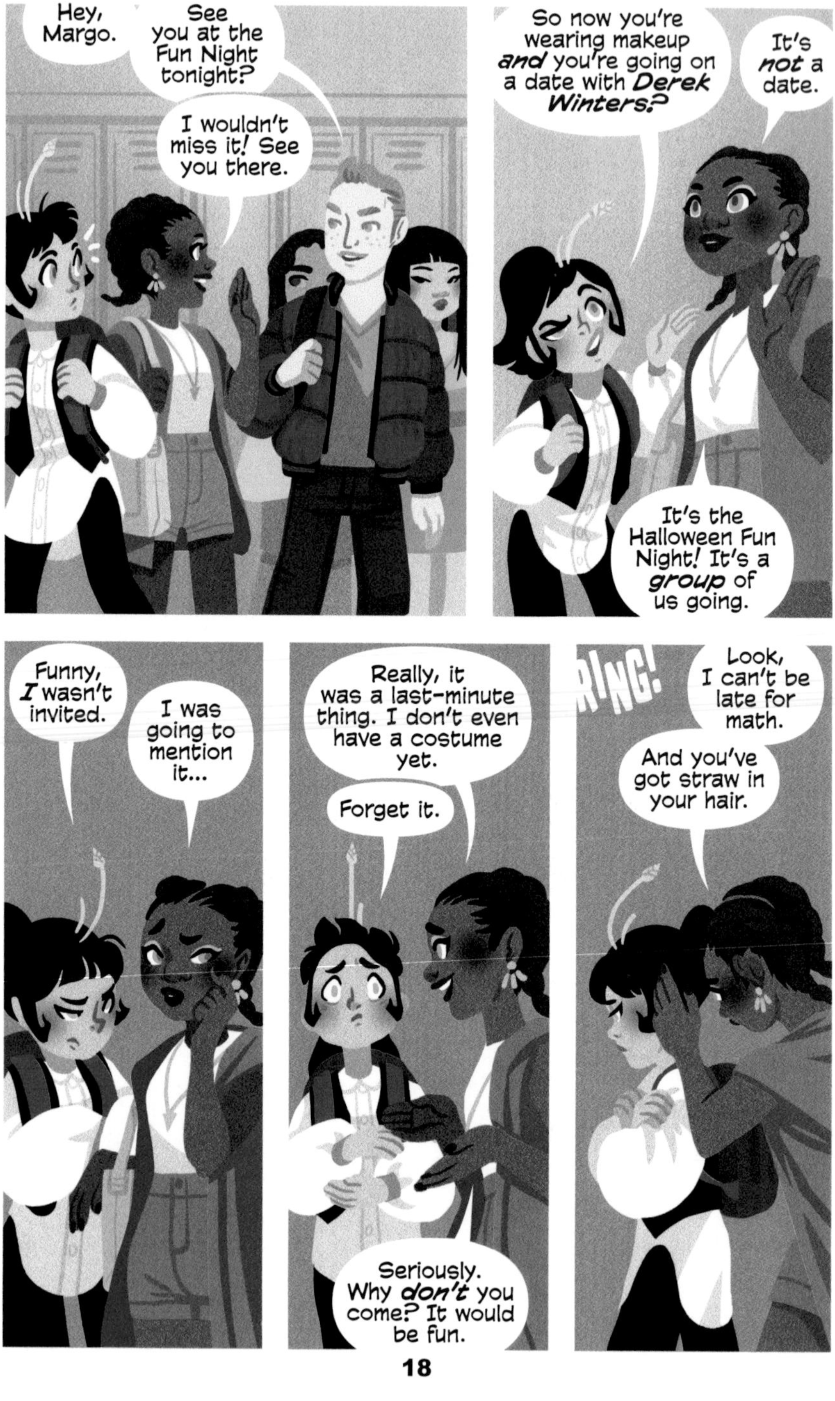
Hey, Margo.
See you at the Fun Night tonight?
I wouldn't miss it! See you there.
So now you're wearing makeup *and* you're going on a date with *Derek Winters?*
It's *not* a date.
It's the Halloween Fun Night! It's a *group* of us going.
Funny, *I* wasn't invited.
I was going to mention it...
Really, it was a last-minute thing. I don't even have a costume yet.
Forget it.
Seriously. Why *don't* you come? It would be fun.
RING!
Look, I can't be late for math.
And you've got straw in your hair.

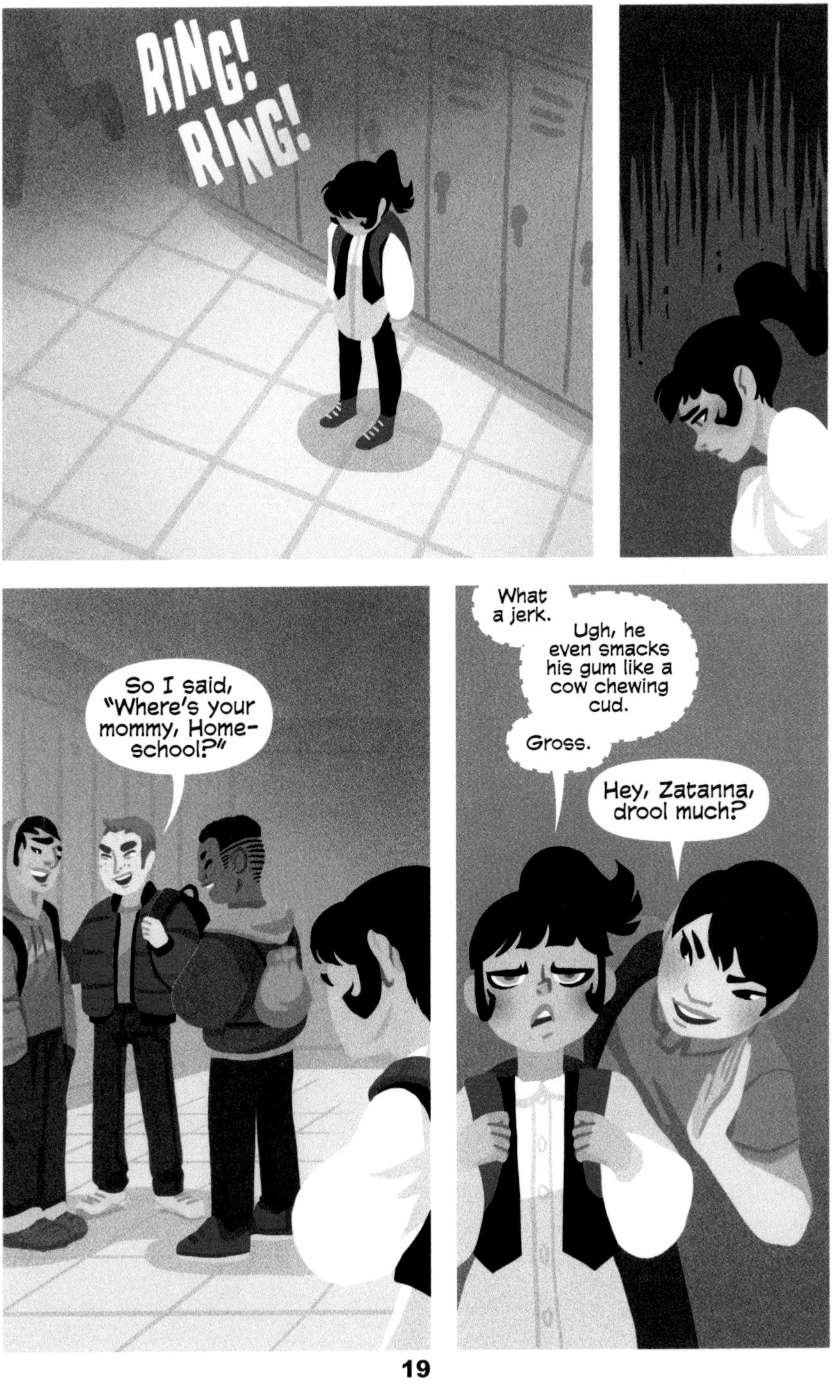
RING!
RING!
So I said, "Where's your mommy, Home-school?"
What a jerk.
Ugh, he even smacks his gum like a cow chewing cud.
Gross.
Hey, Zatanna, drool much?

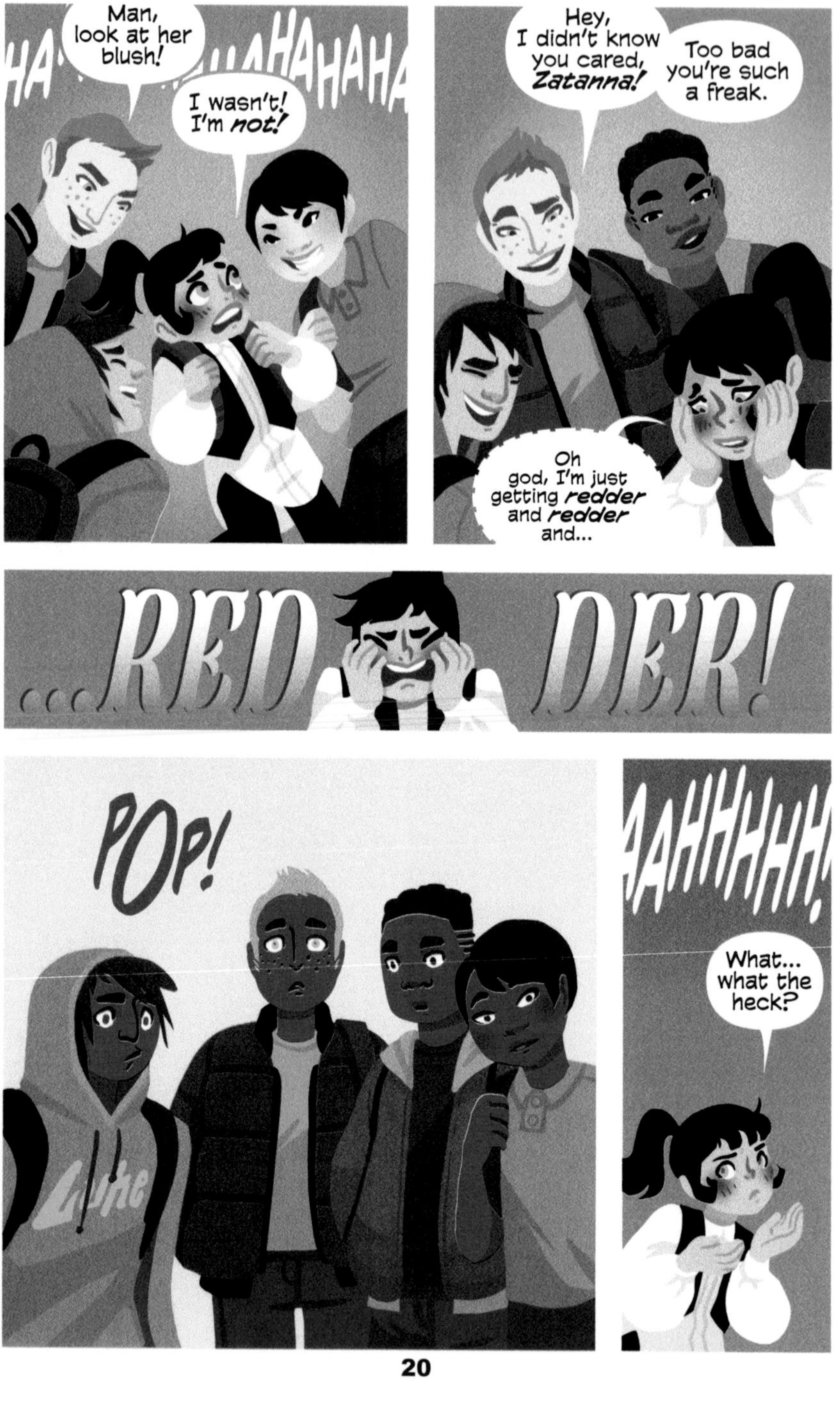
HAHAHAHAHA
Man, look at her blush!
I wasn't! I'm *not!*
Hey, I didn't know you cared, *Zatanna!*
Too bad you're such a freak.
Oh god, I'm just getting *redder* and *redder* and...
...RED DER!
POP!
AHHHHHH!
What... what the heck?

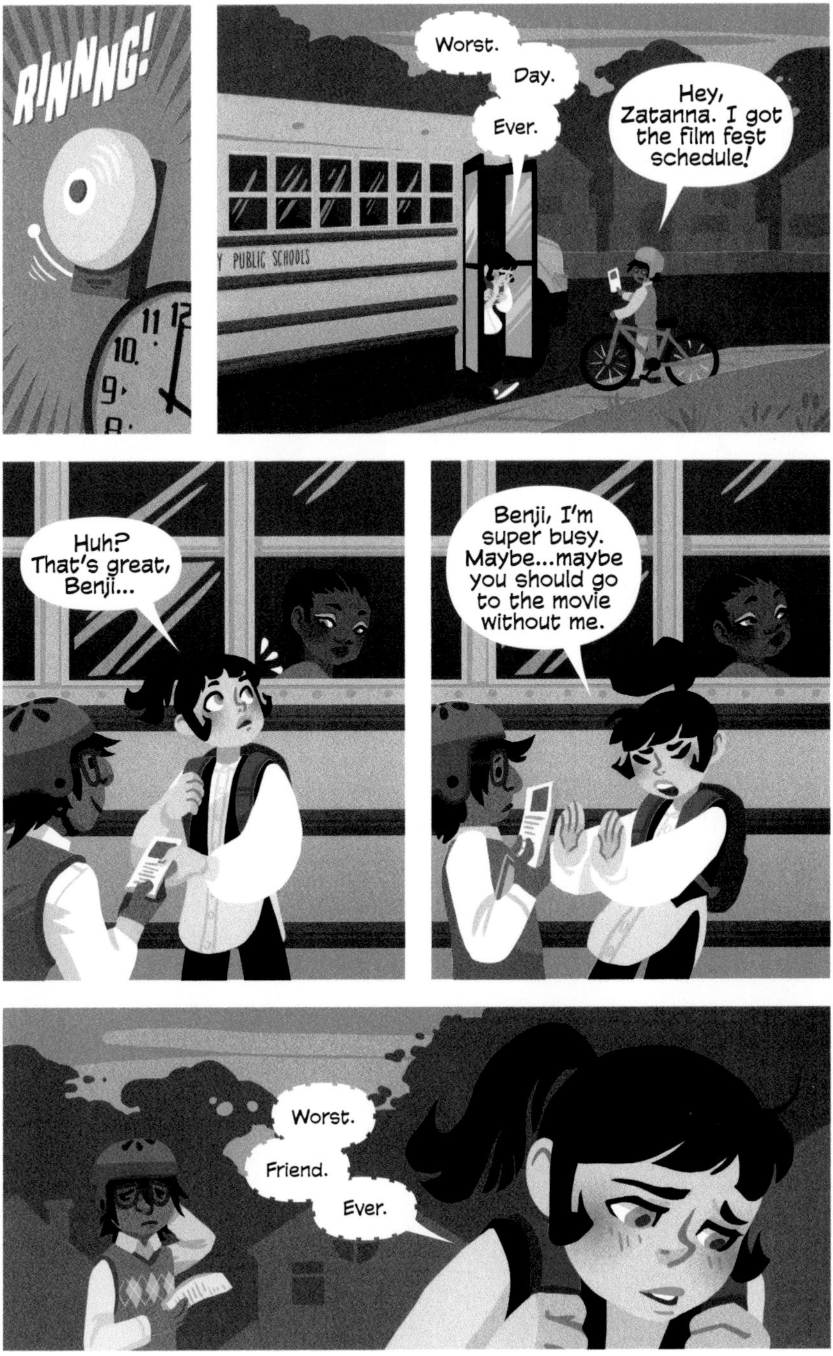

RINNNG!
PUBLIC SCHOOLS
Worst.
Day.
Ever.
Hey, Zatanna. I got the film fest schedule!
Huh? That's great, Benji...
Benji, I'm super busy. Maybe...maybe you should go to the movie without me.
Worst.
Friend.
Ever.

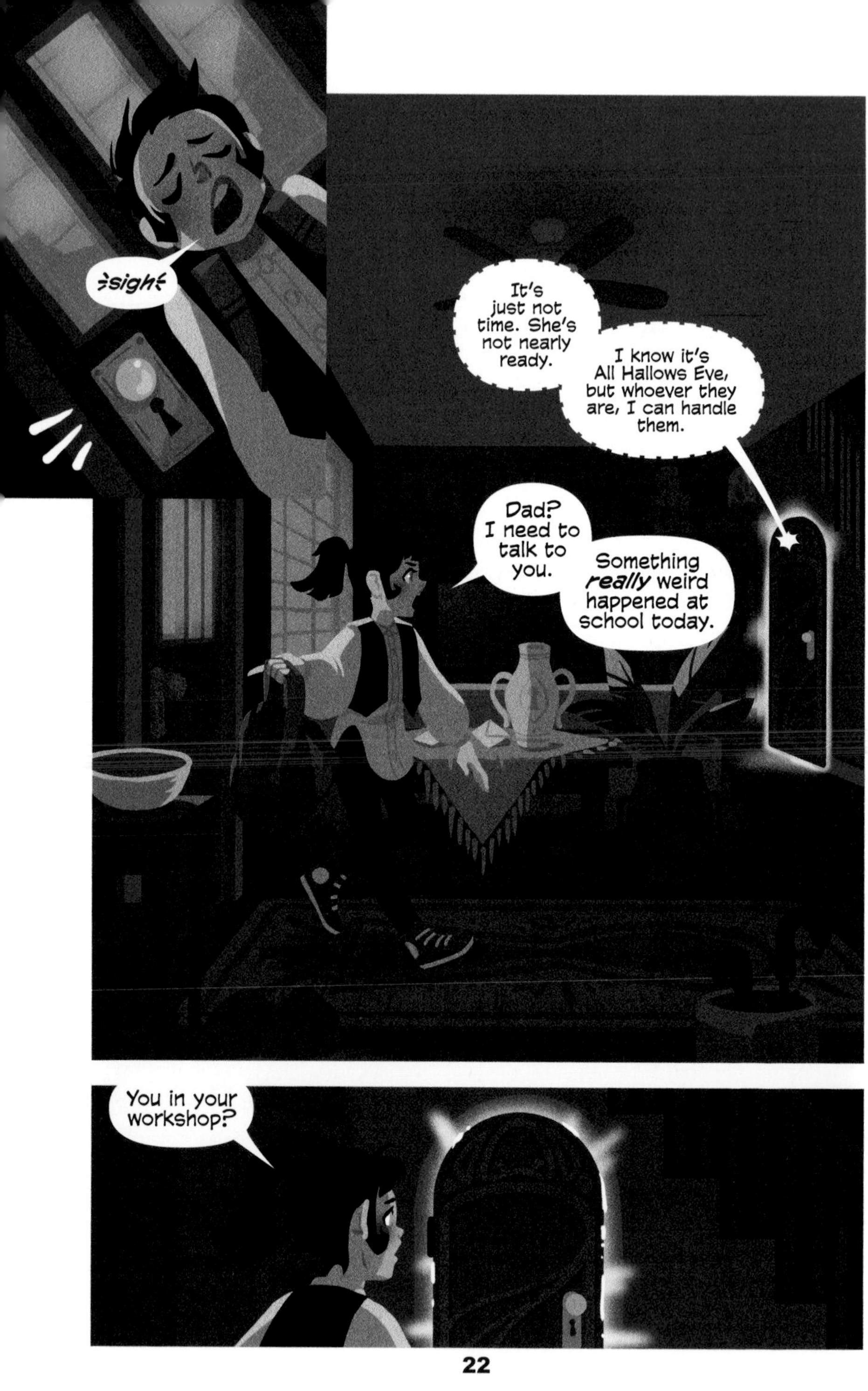
sigh
It's just not time. She's not nearly ready.
I know it's All Hallows Eve, but whoever they are, I can handle them.
Dad? I need to talk to you.
Something *really* weird happened at school today.
You in your workshop?

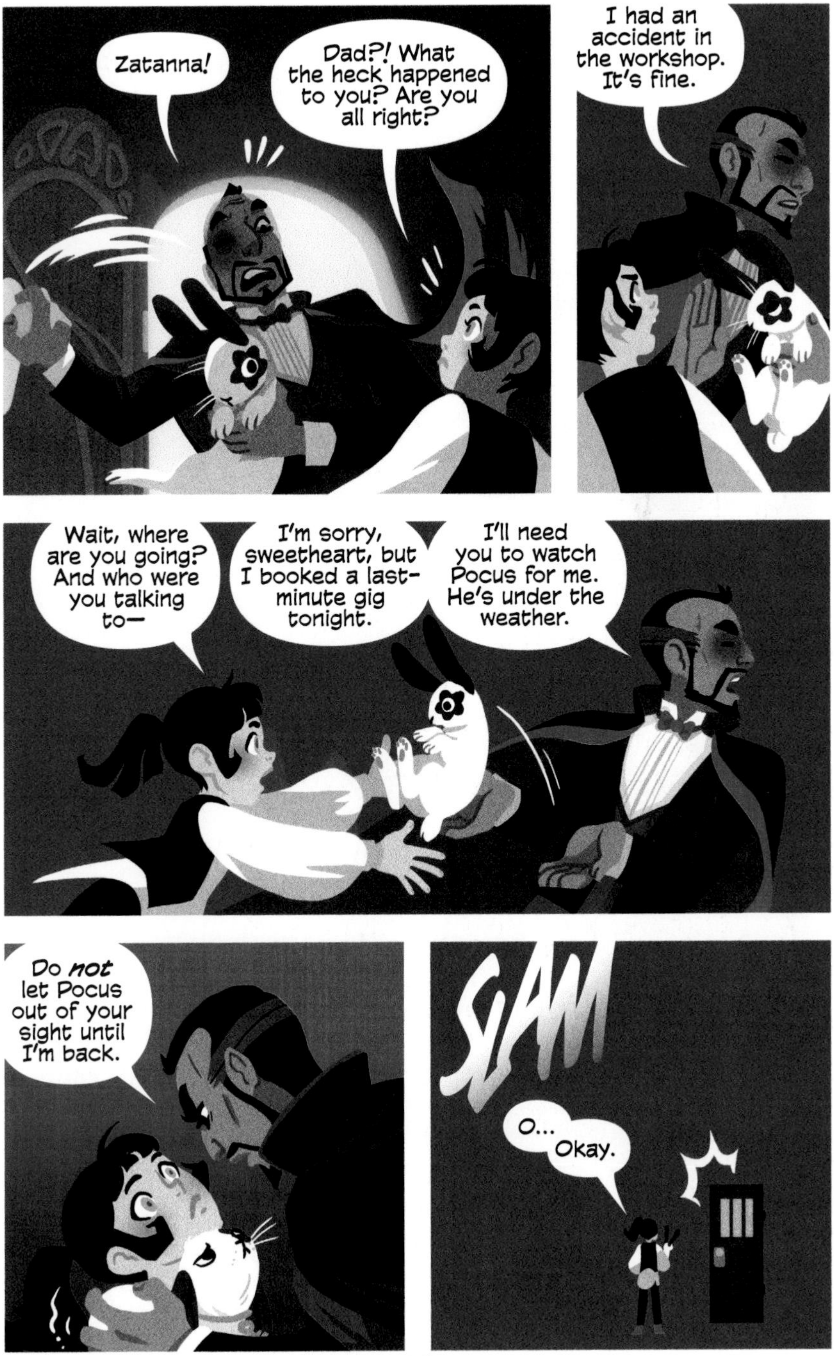
Zatanna!
Dad?! What the heck happened to you? Are you all right?
I had an accident in the workshop. It's fine.
Wait, where are you going? And who were you talking to—
I'm sorry, sweetheart, but I booked a last-minute gig tonight.
I'll need you to watch Pocus for me. He's under the weather.
Do ***not*** let Pocus out of your sight until I'm back.
SLAM
O... Okay.

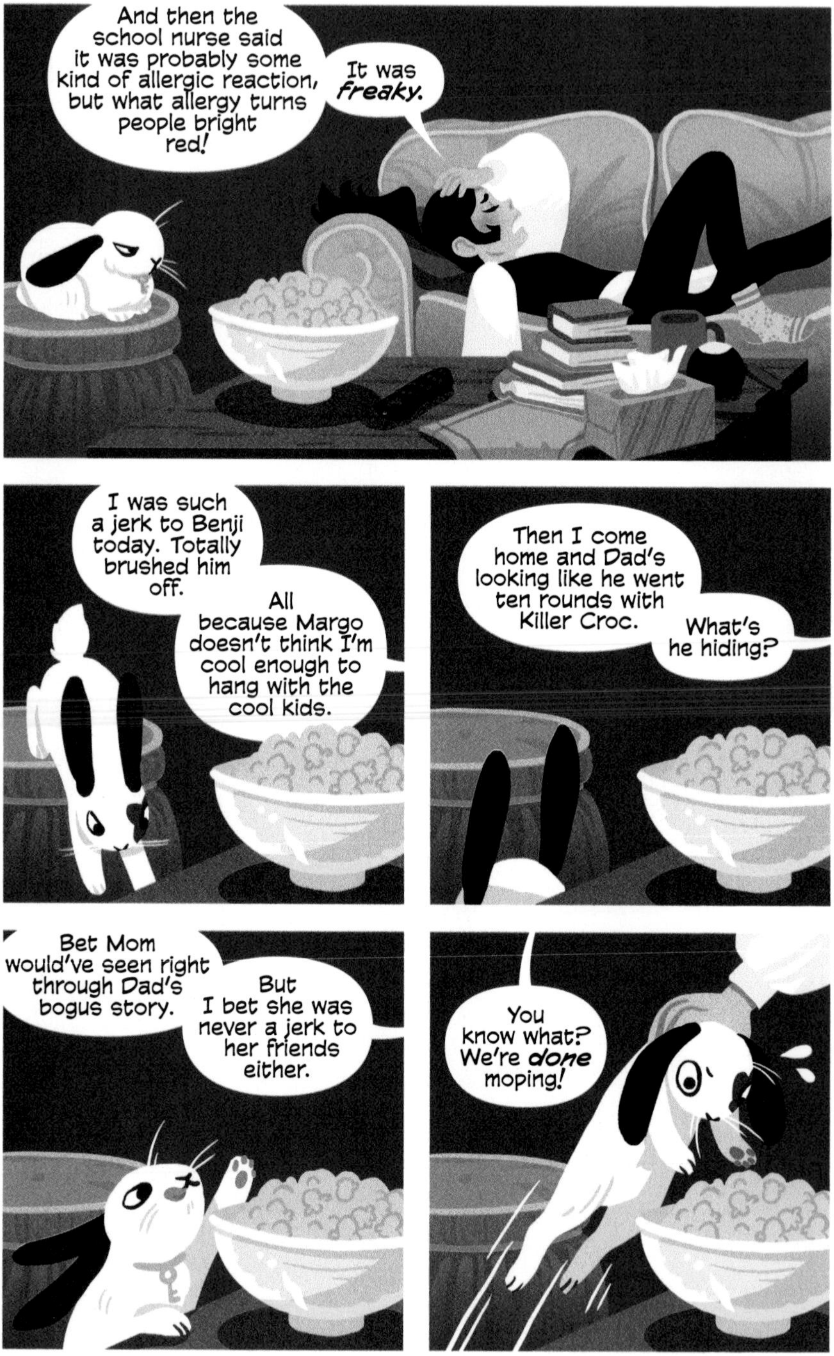
And then the school nurse said it was probably some kind of allergic reaction, but what allergy turns people bright red!
It was *freaky.*
I was such a jerk to Benji today. Totally brushed him off.
All because Margo doesn't think I'm cool enough to hang with the cool kids.
Then I come home and Dad's looking like he went ten rounds with Killer Croc.
What's he hiding?
Bet Mom would've seen right through Dad's bogus story.
But I bet she was never a jerk to her friends either.
You know what? We're *done* moping!

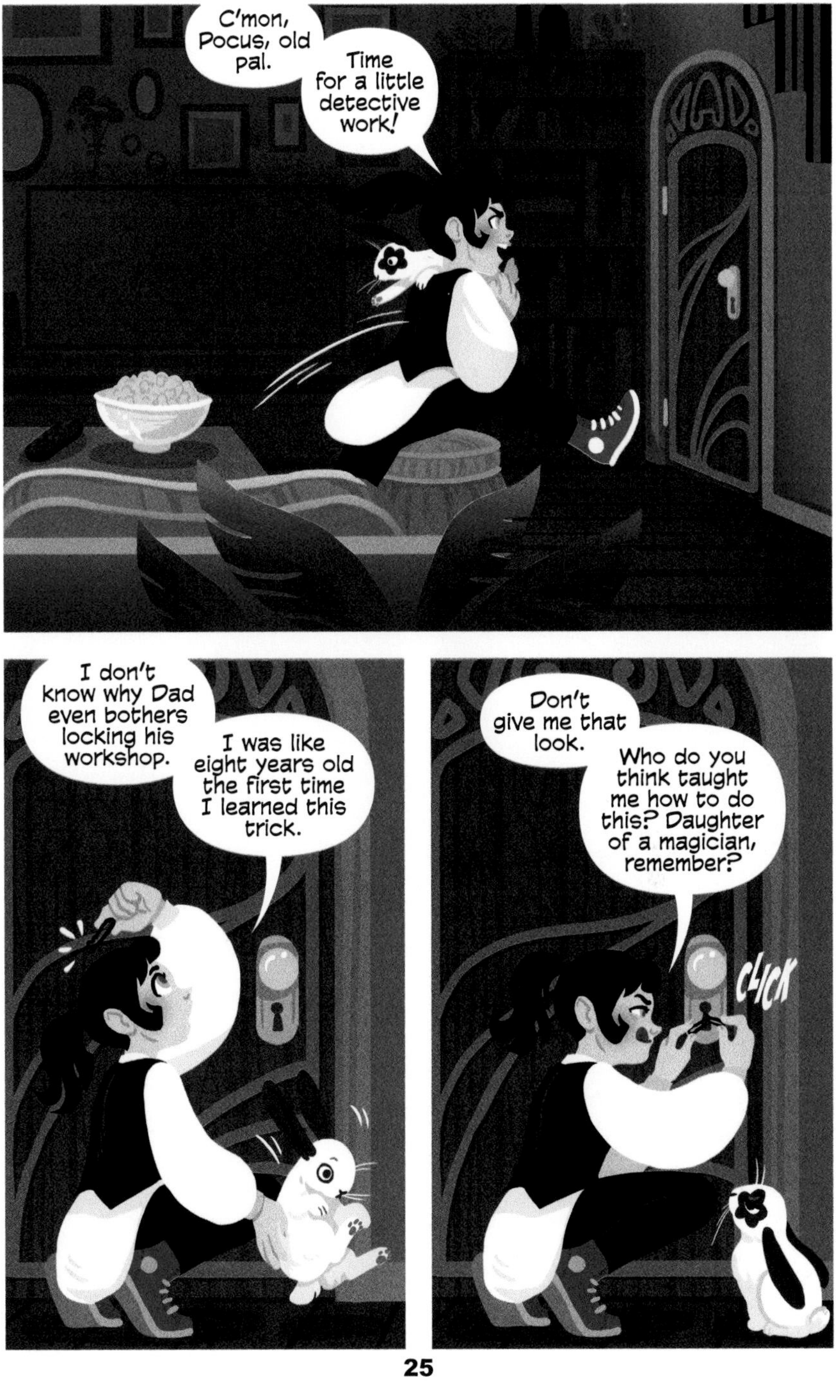
C'mon, Pocus, old pal.
Time for a little detective work!
I don't know why Dad even bothers locking his workshop.
I was like eight years old the first time I learned this trick.
Don't give me that look.
Who do you think taught me how to do this? Daughter of a magician, remember?
CLICK

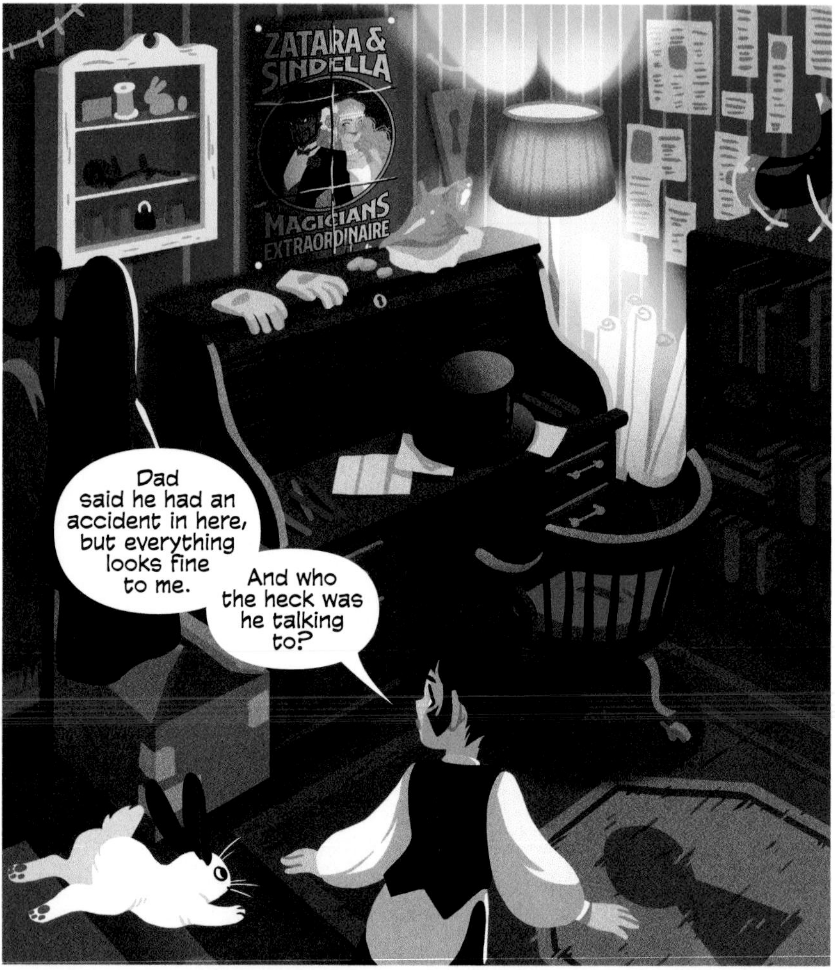
ZATARA & SINDELLA
MAGICIANS EXTRAORDINAIRE
Dad said he had an accident in here, but everything looks fine to me.
And who the heck was he talking to?

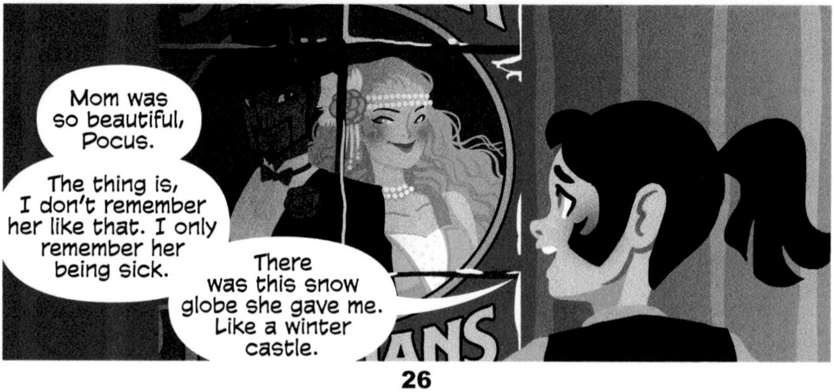
Mom was so beautiful, Pocus.
The thing is, I don't remember her like that. I only remember her being sick.
There was this snow globe she gave me. Like a winter castle.

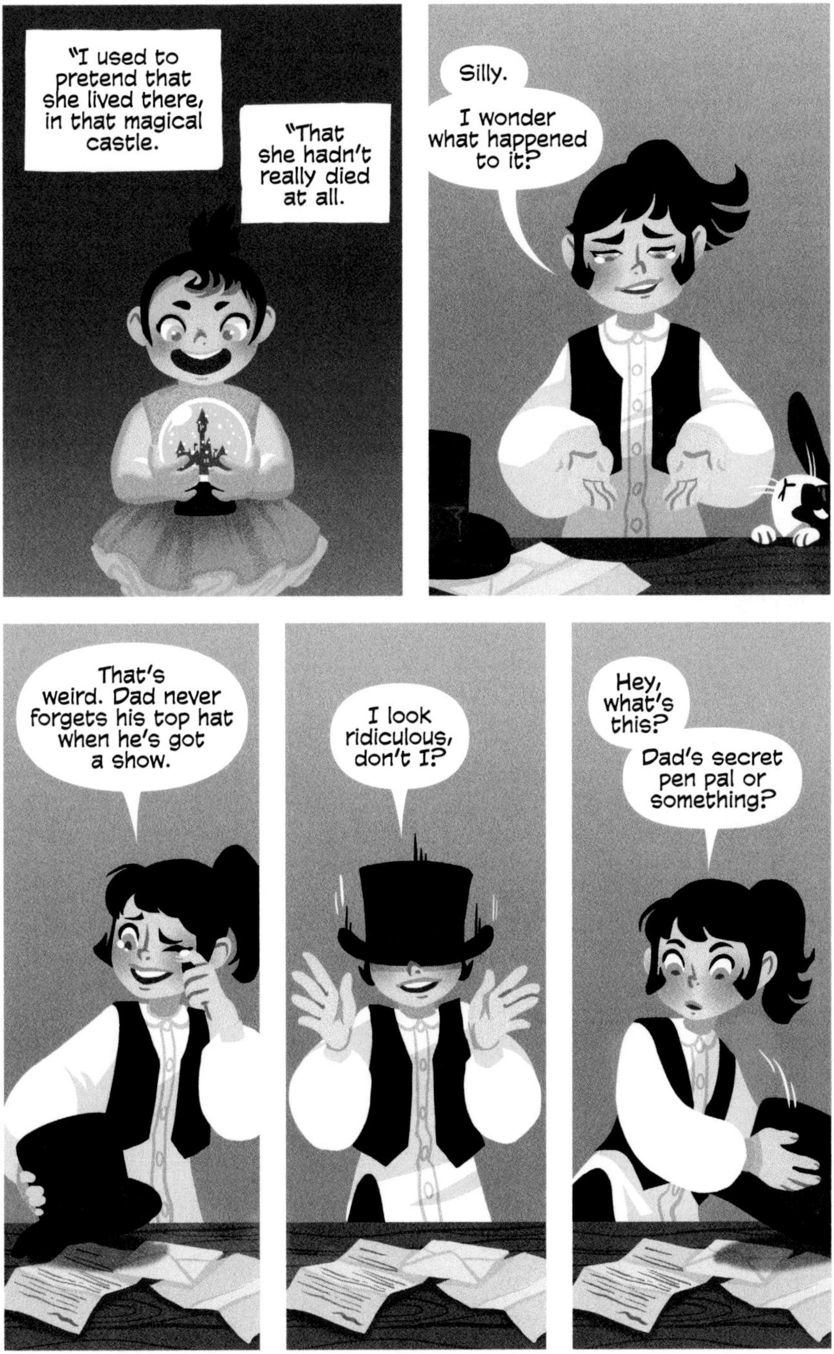
"I used to pretend that she lived there, in that magical castle.
"That she hadn't really died at all.
Silly.
I wonder what happened to it?
That's weird. Dad never forgets his top hat when he's got a show.
I look ridiculous, don't I?
Hey, what's this?
Dad's secret pen pal or something?

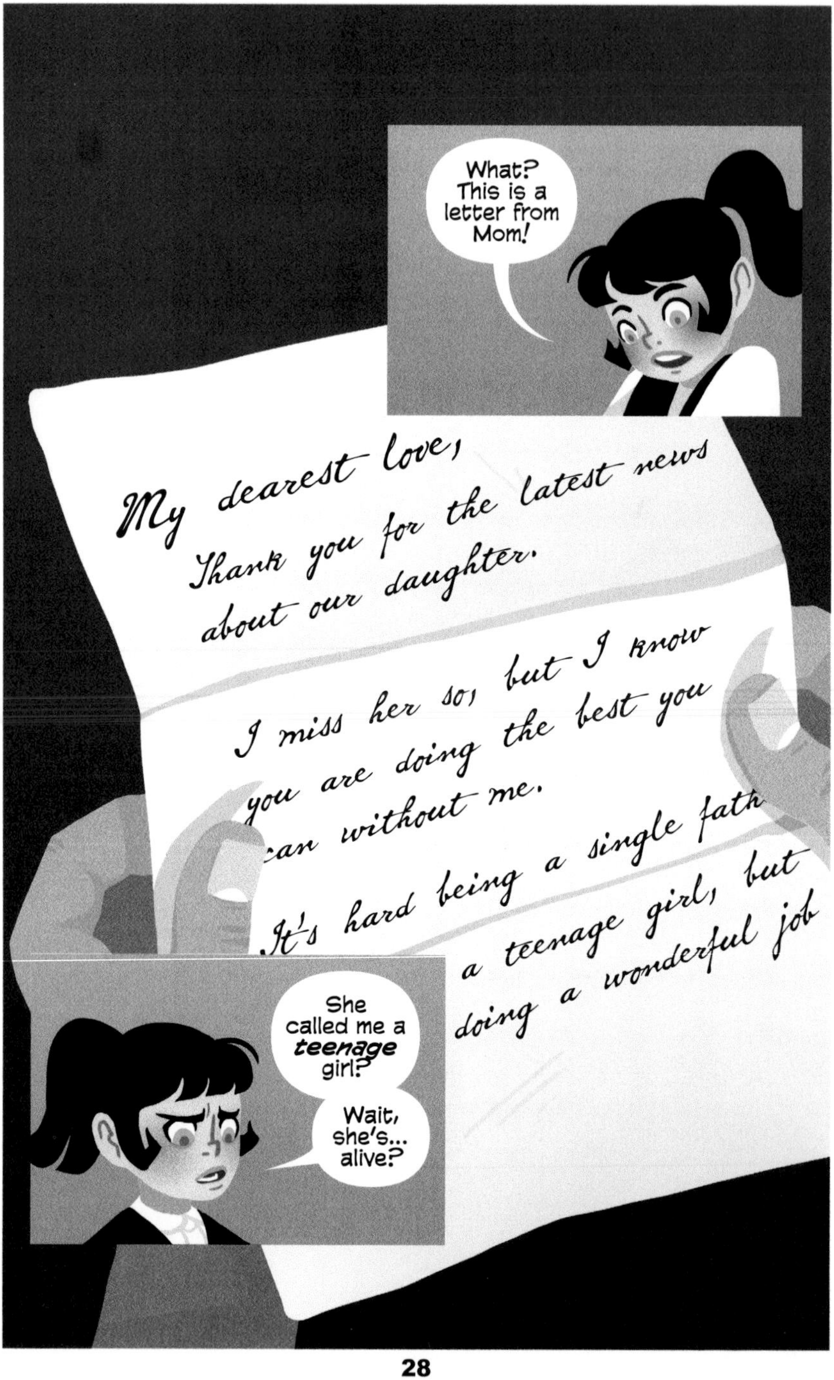
What? This is a letter from Mom!
My dearest love,
Thank you for the latest news about our daughter.
I miss her so, but I know you are doing the best you can without me.
It's hard being a single fath
a teenage girl, but
doing a wonderful job
She called me a ***teenage*** girl?
Wait, she's... alive?

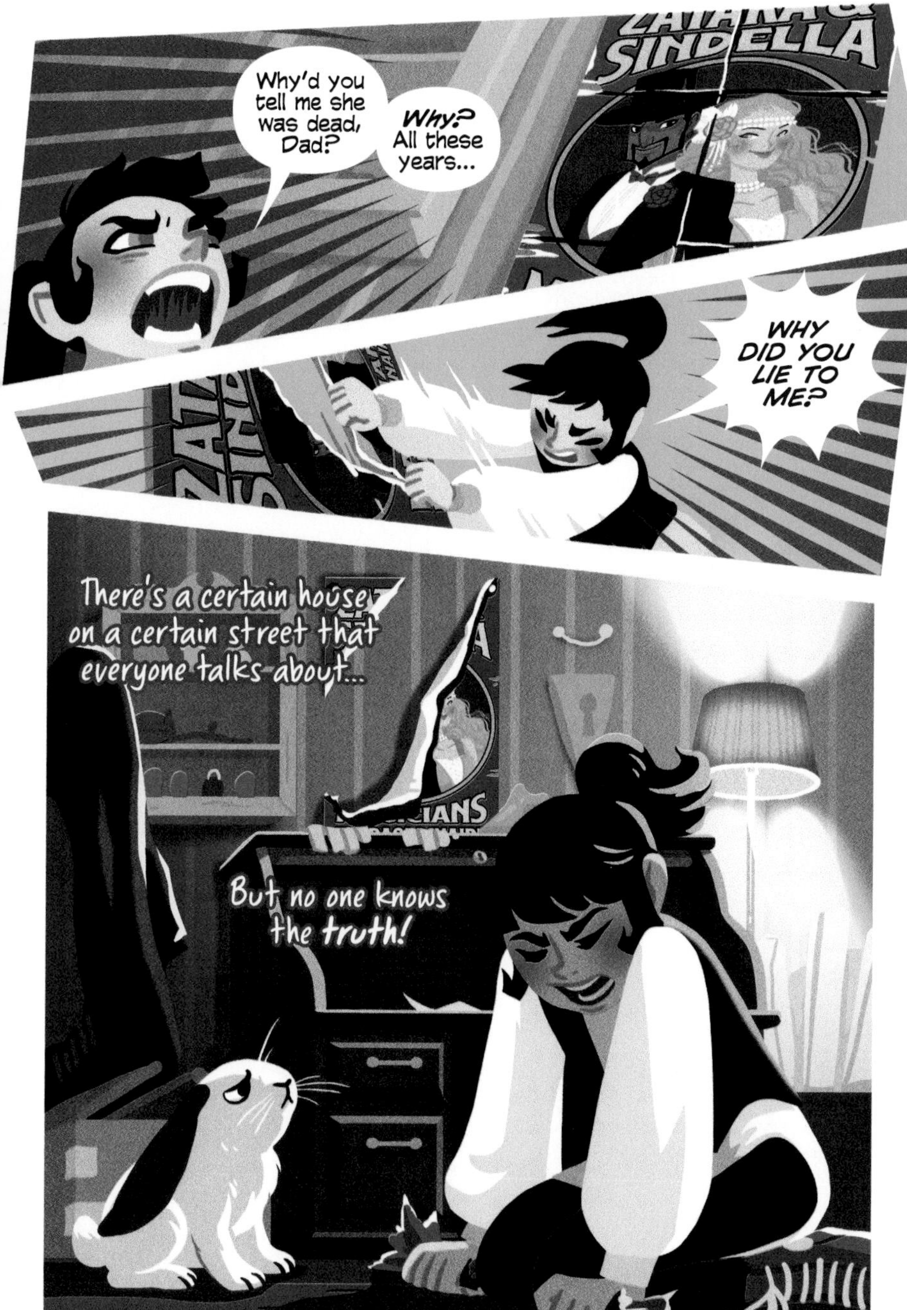
Why'd you tell me she was dead, Dad?
Why? All these years...
WHY DID YOU LIE TO ME?
There's a certain house on a certain street that everyone talks about...
But no one knows the truth!

Chapter Two

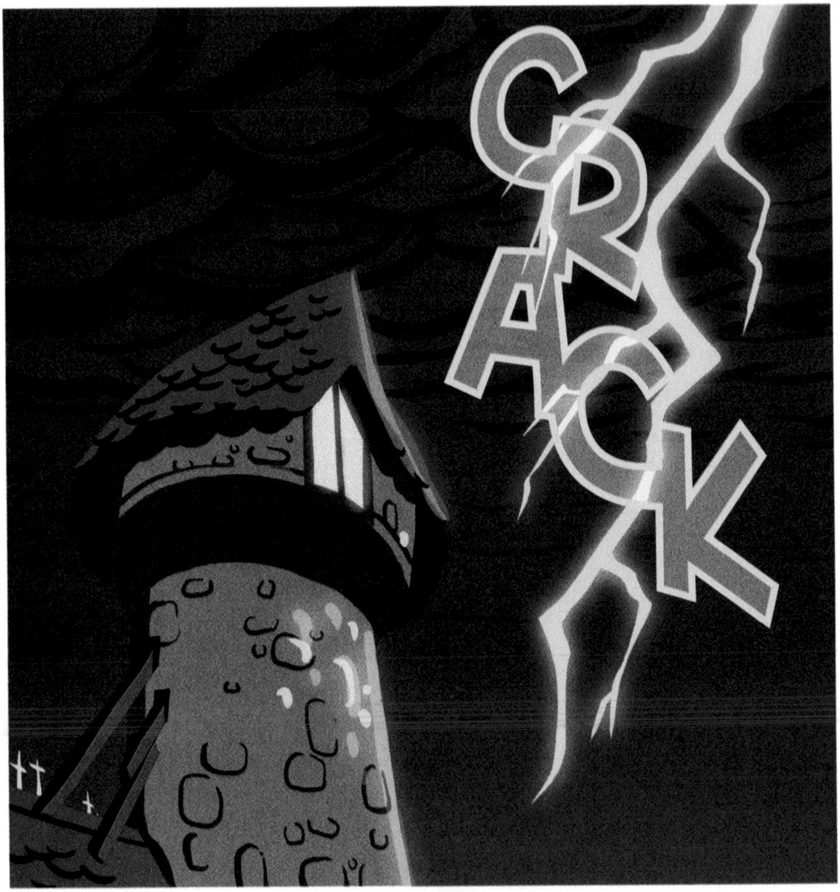
CRACK

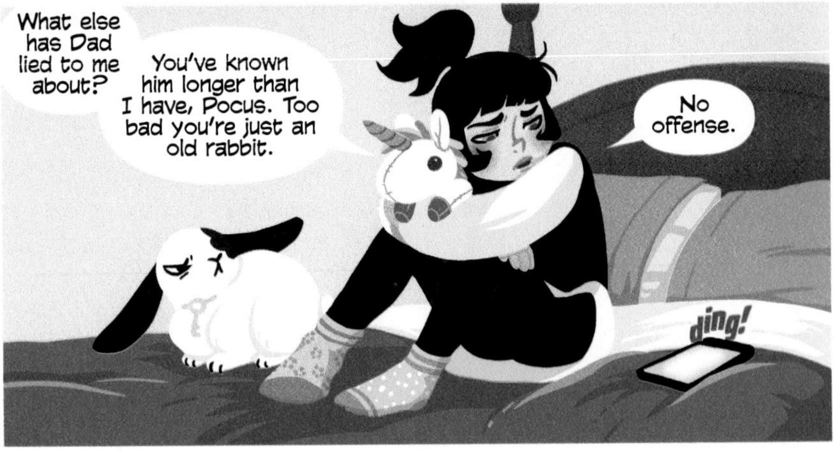
What else has Dad lied to me about?
You've known him longer than I have, Pocus. Too bad you're just an old rabbit.
No offense.
ding!

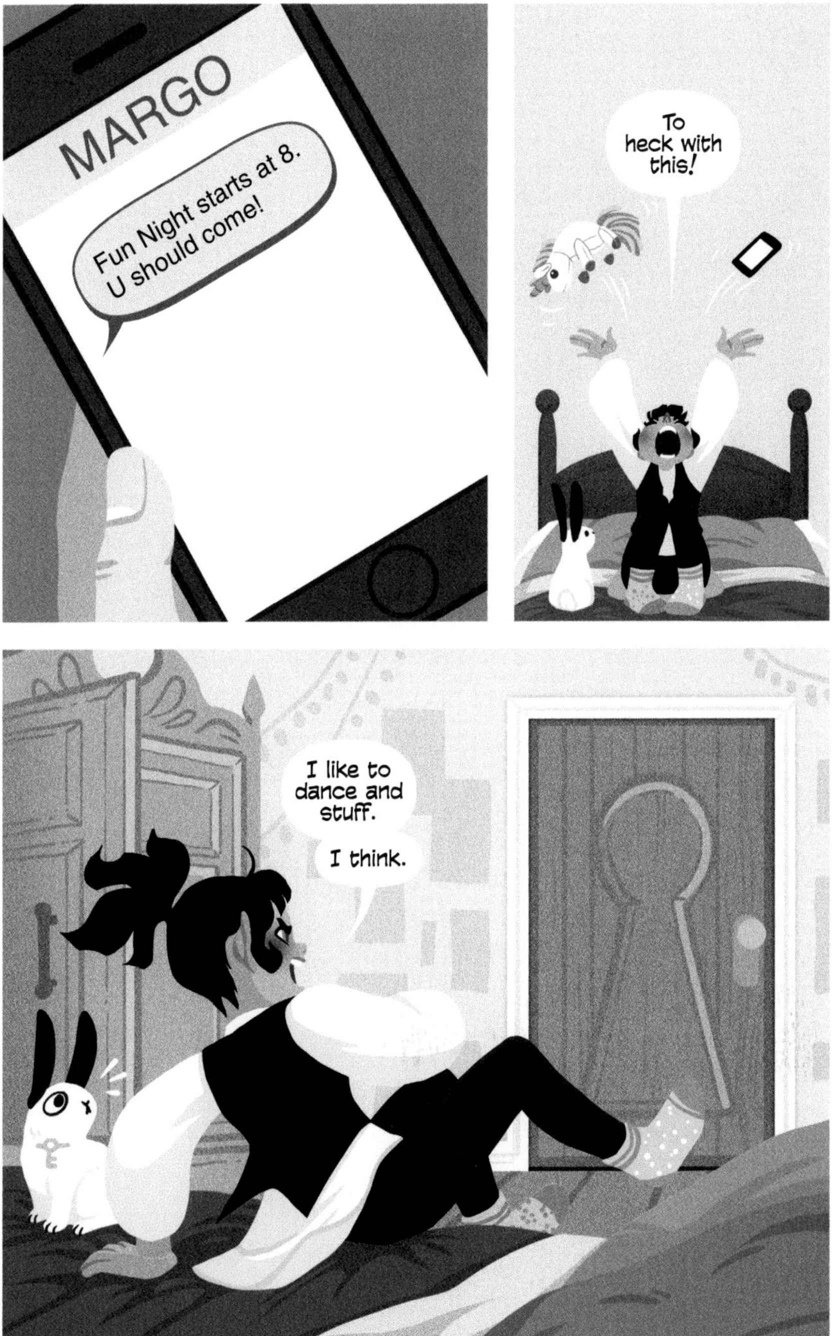
MARGO
Fun Night starts at 8. U should come!
To heck with this!
I like to dance and stuff.
I think.

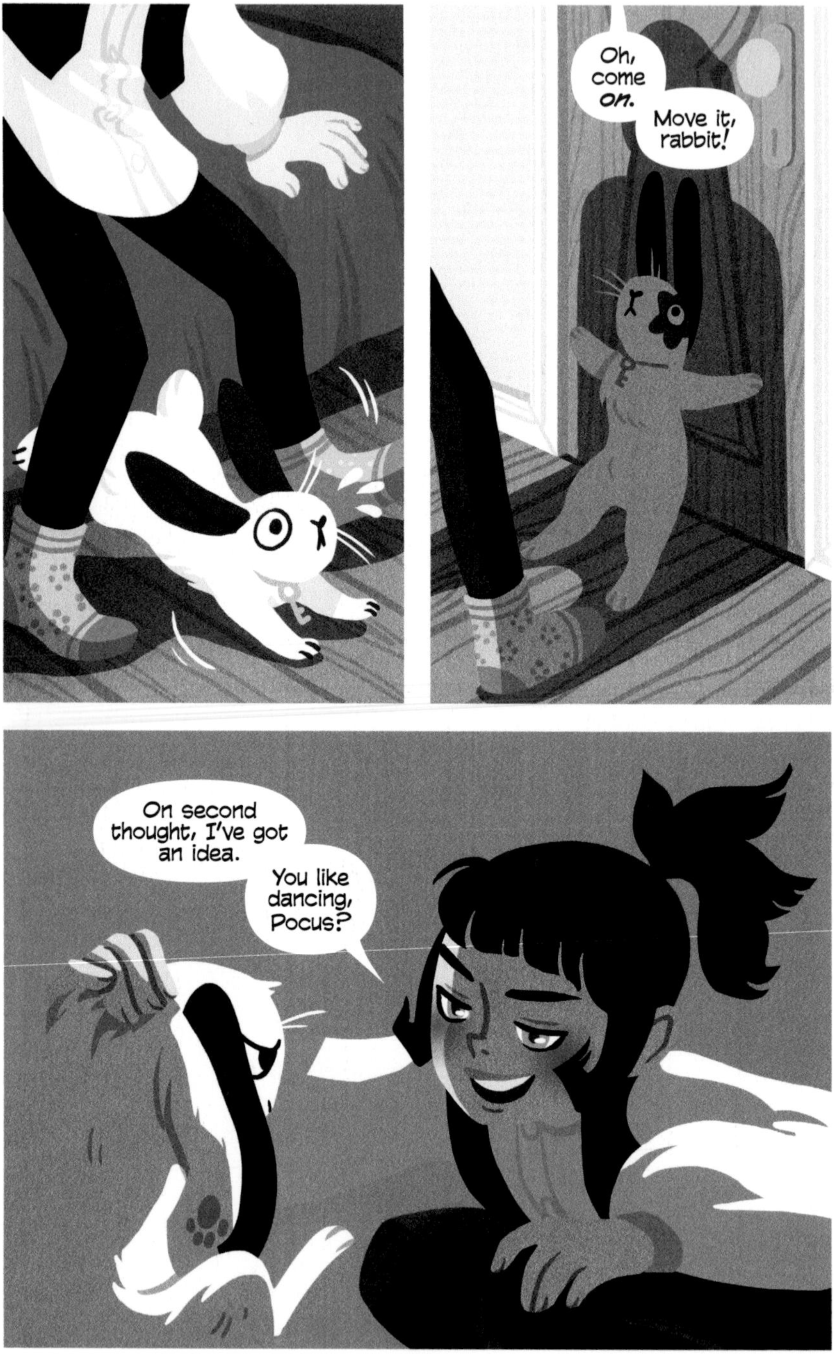
Oh, come on.
Move it, rabbit!
On second thought, I've got an idea.
You like dancing, Pocus?

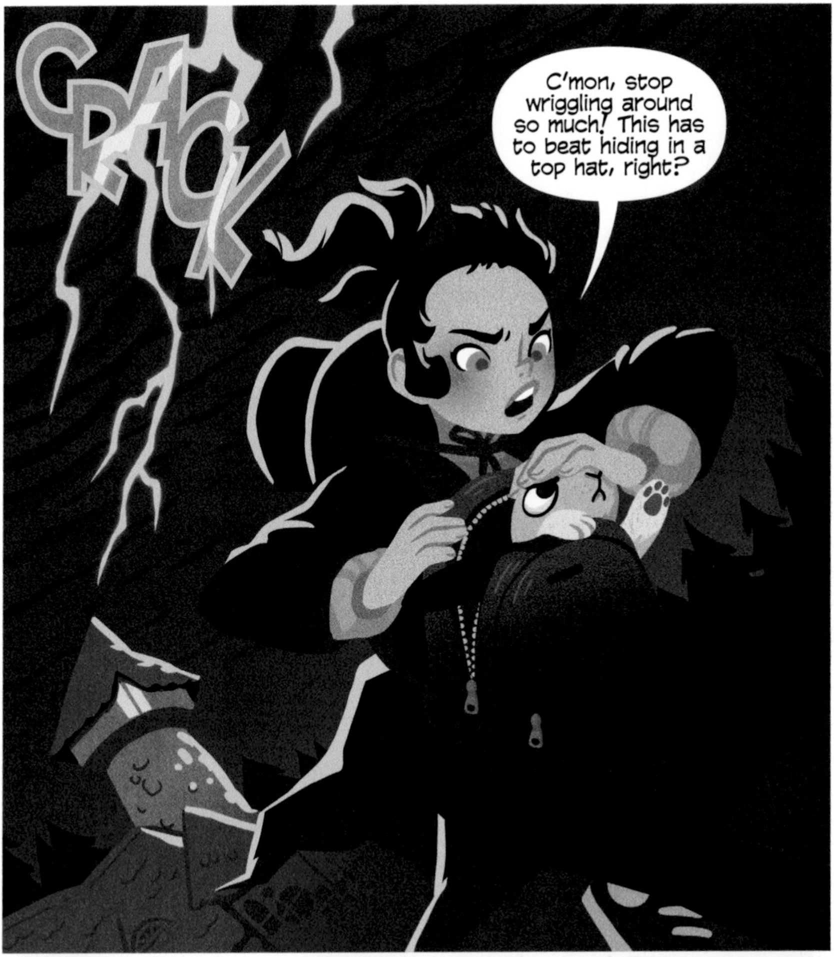
CRACK
C'mon, stop wriggling around so much! This has to beat hiding in a top hat, right?

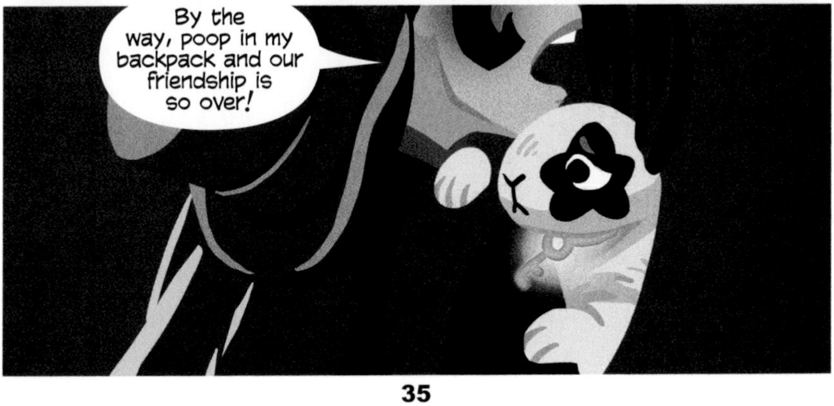
By the way, poop in my backpack and our friendship is so over!

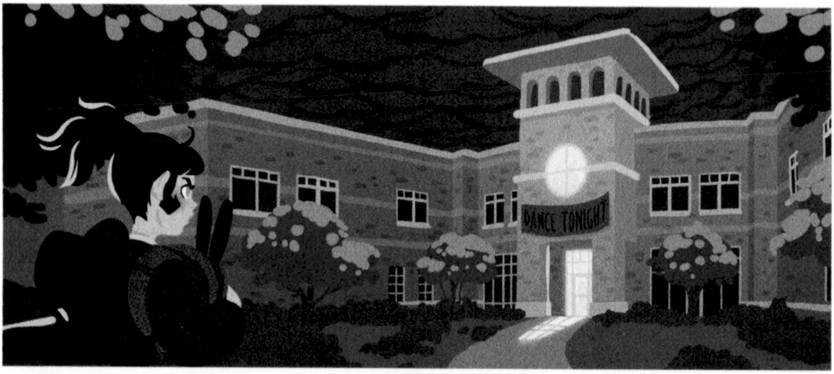
DANCE TONIGHT

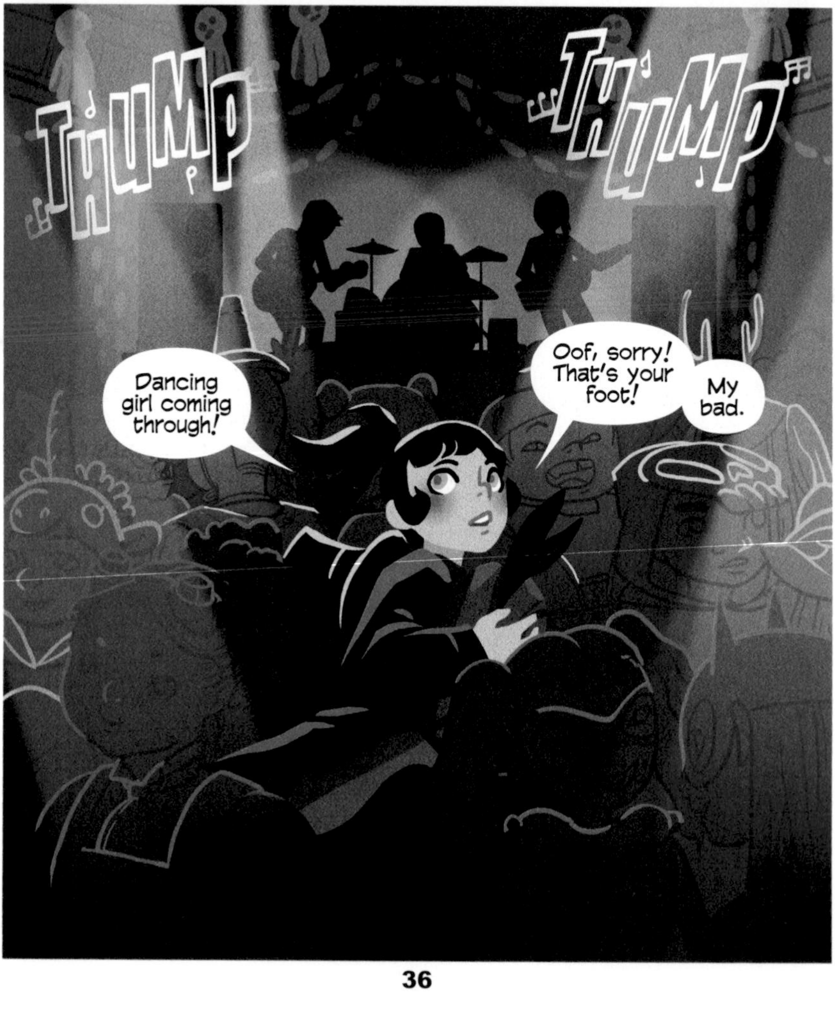
THUMP
THUMP
Dancing girl coming through!
Oof, sorry! That's your foot!
My bad.

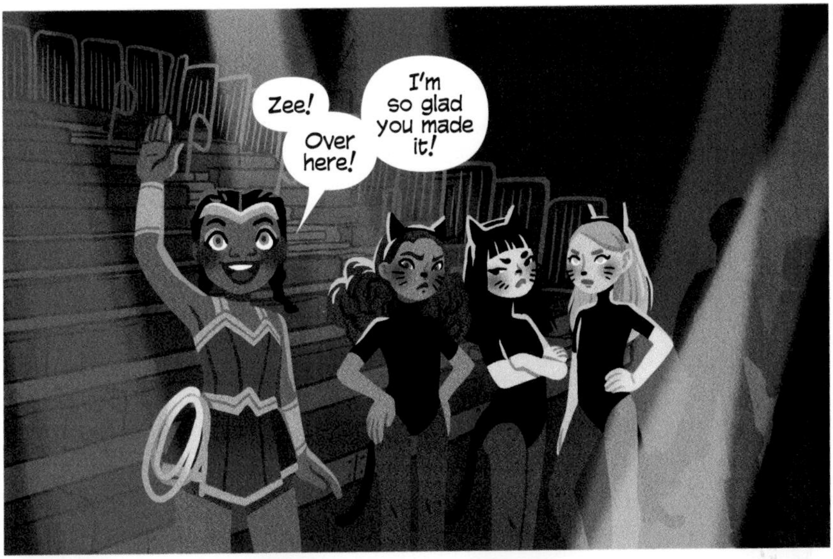
Zee!
Over here!
I'm so glad you made it!

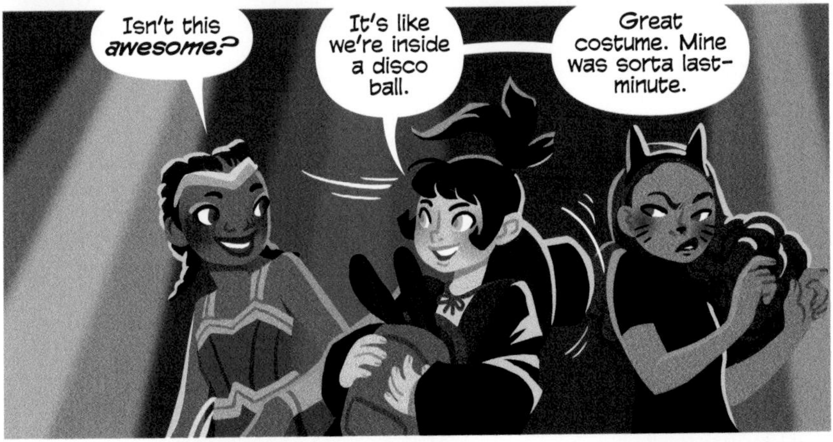
Isn't this *awesome?*
It's like we're inside a disco ball.
Great costume. Mine was sorta last-minute.

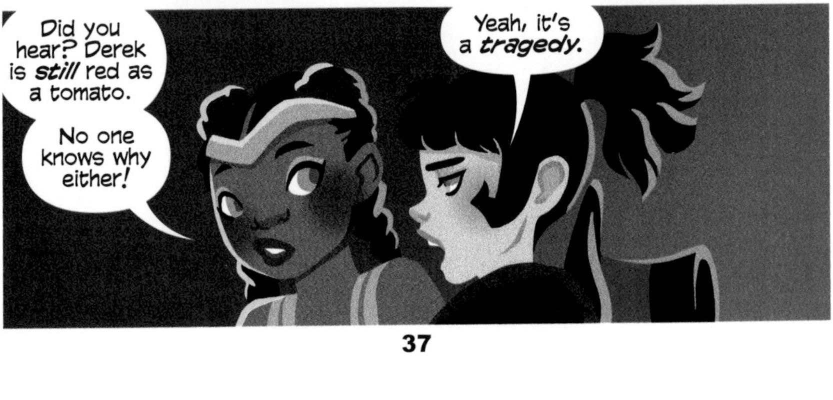
Did you hear? Derek is *still* red as a tomato.
No one knows why either!
Yeah, it's a *tragedy*.

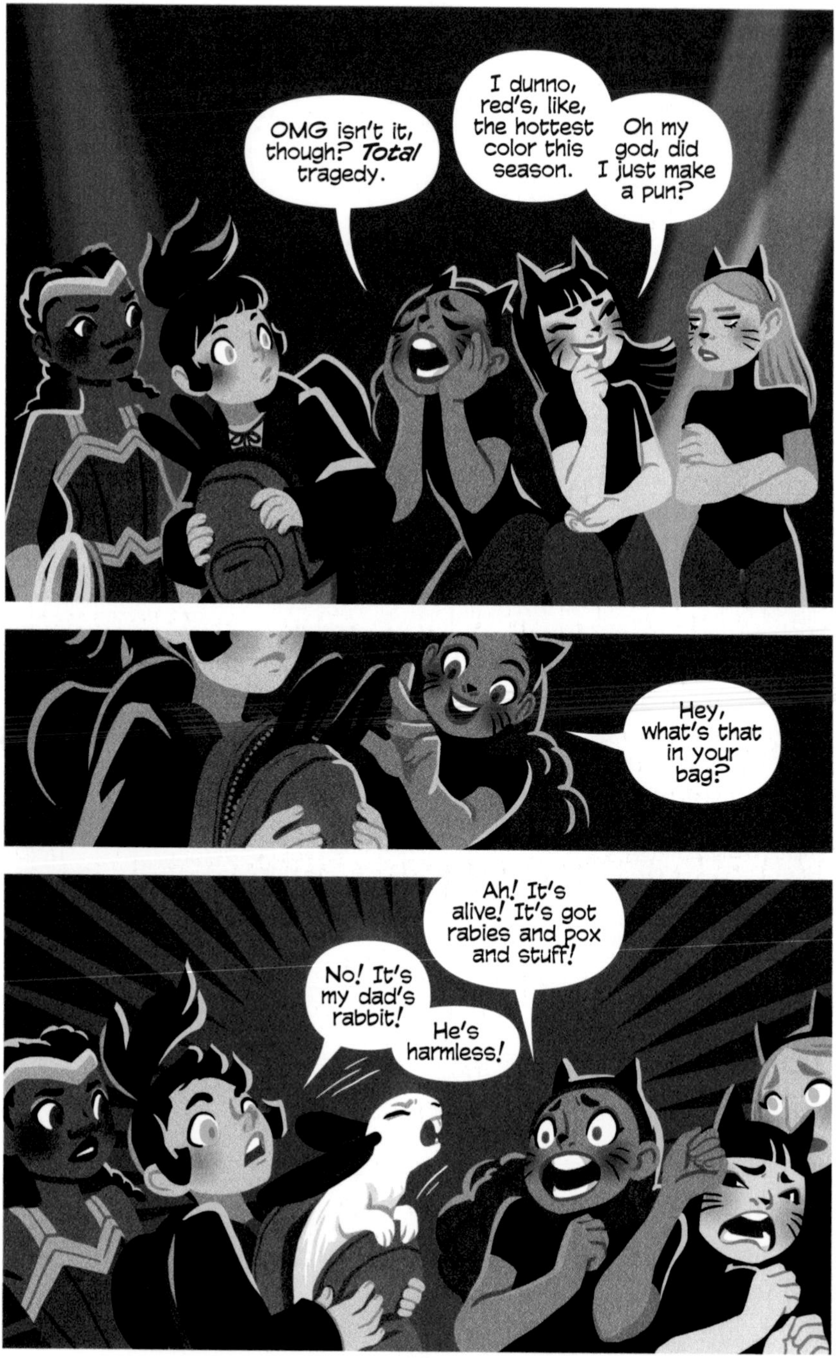
OMG isn't it, though? *Total* tragedy.
I dunno, red's, like, the hottest color this season.
Oh my god, did I just make a pun?
Hey, what's that in your bag?
Ah! It's alive! It's got rabies and pox and stuff!
No! It's my dad's rabbit!
He's harmless!

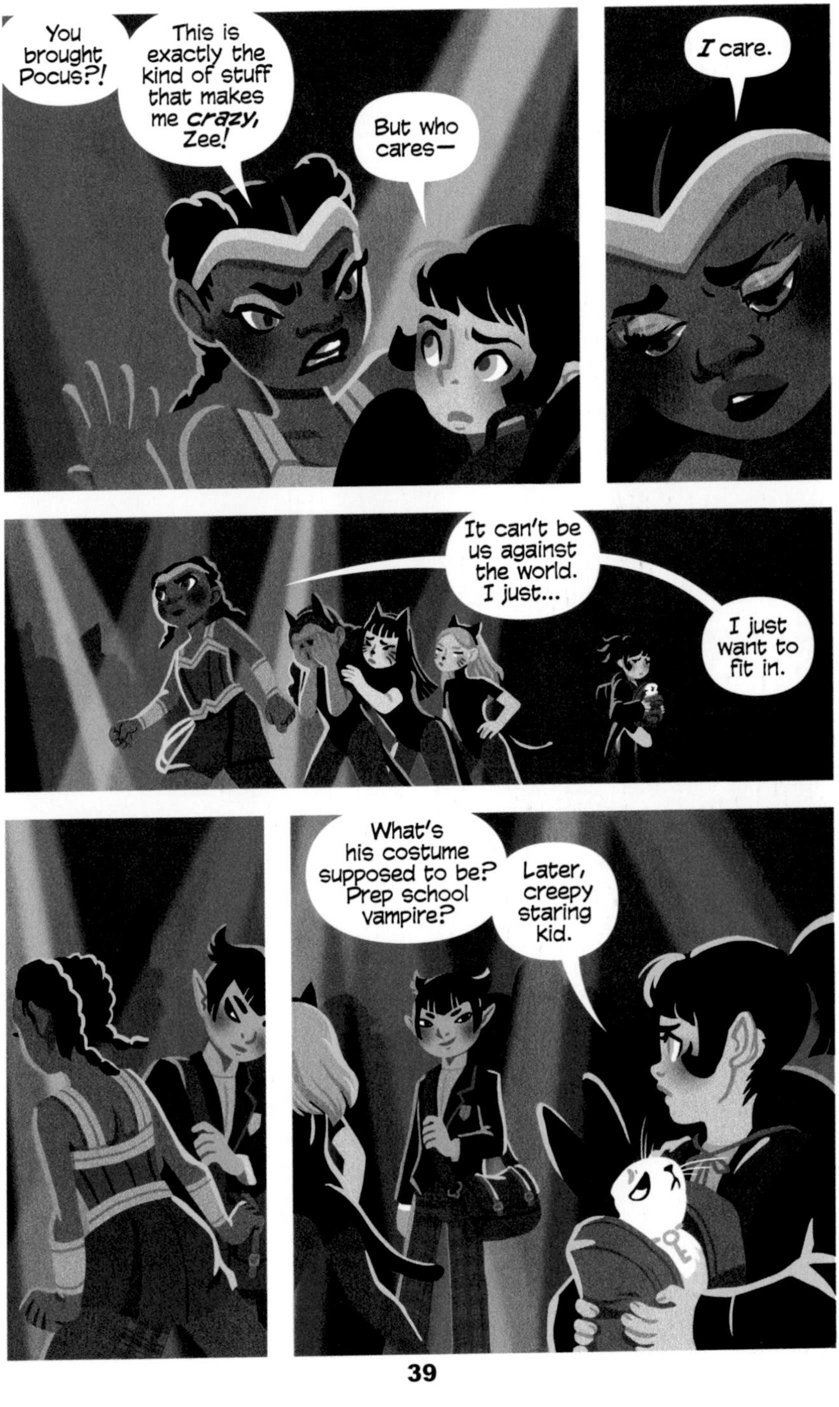
You brought Pocus?!
This is exactly the kind of stuff that makes me *crazy*, Zee!
But who cares—
I care.
It can't be us against the world. I just...
I just want to fit in.
What's his costume supposed to be? Prep school vampire?
Later, creepy staring kid.

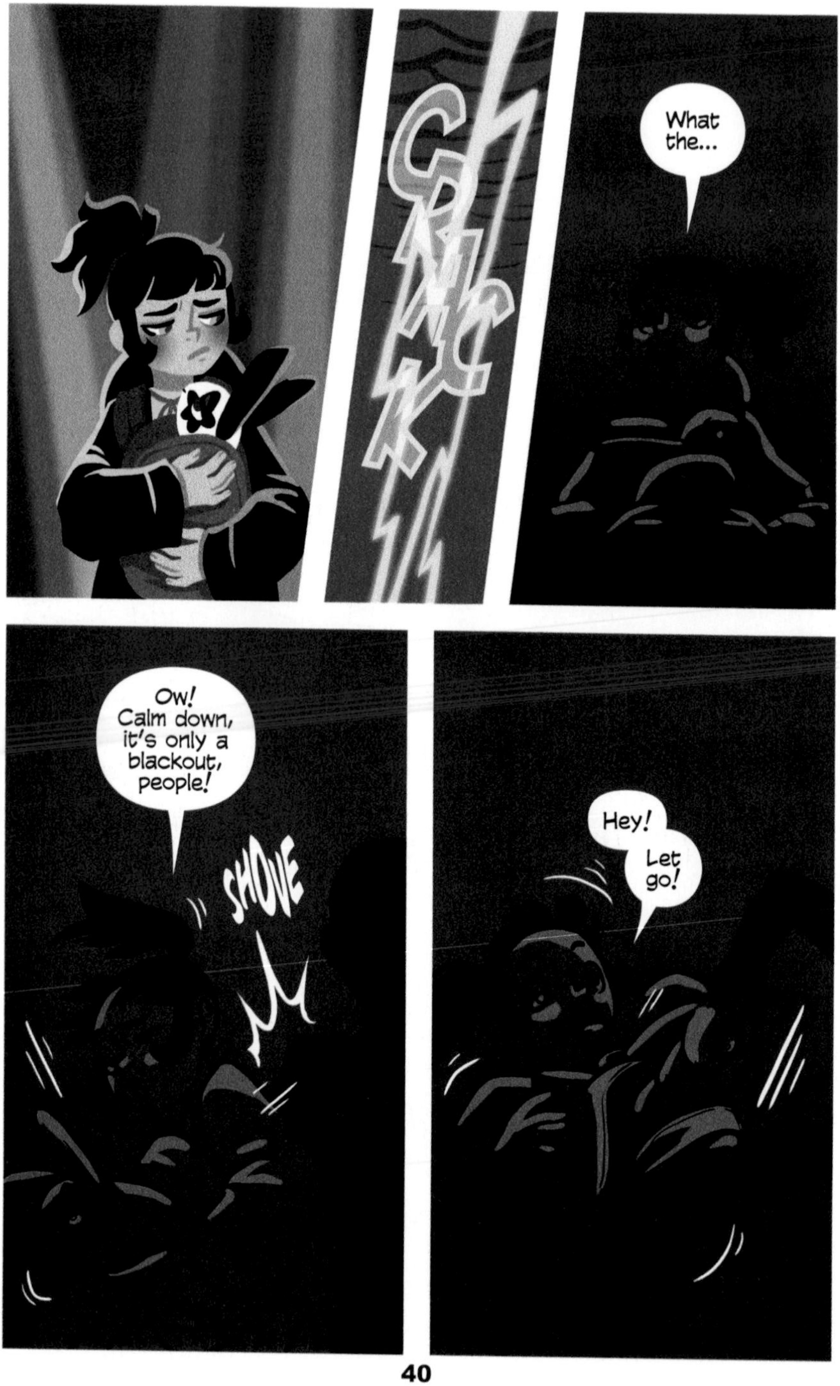
CRACK
What the...
Ow! Calm down, it's only a blackout, people!
SHOVE
Hey!
Let go!

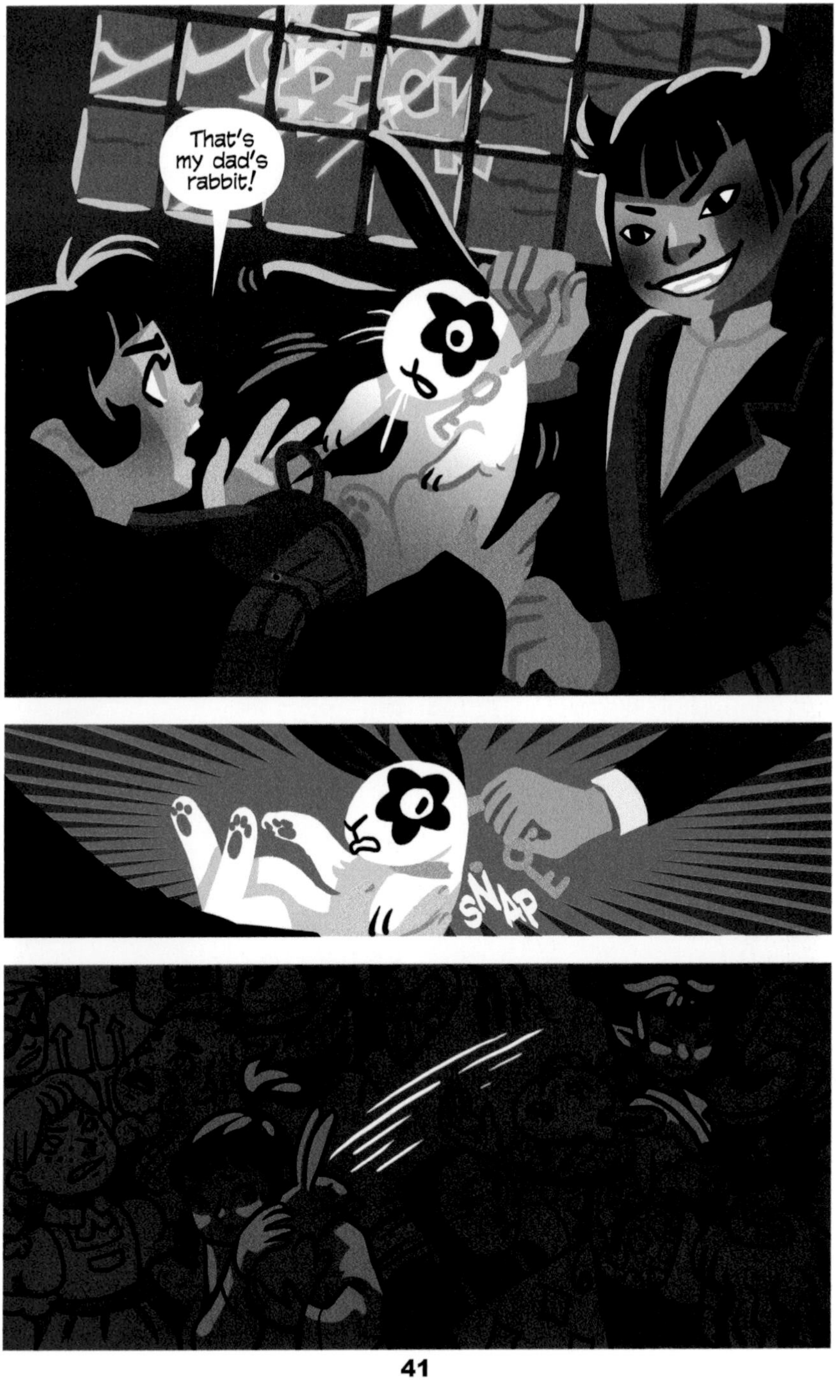

That's my dad's rabbit!
SNAP

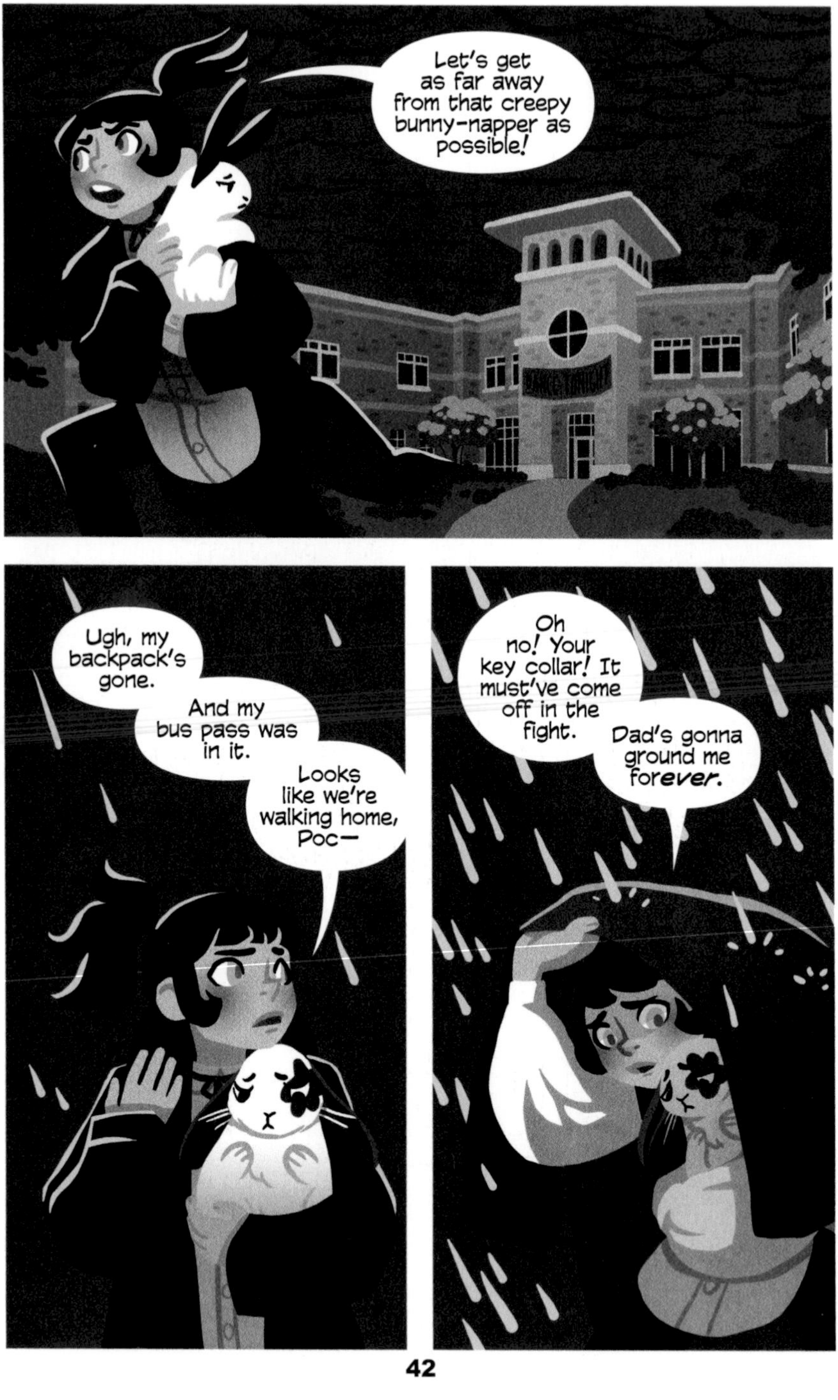
Let's get as far away from that creepy bunny-napper as possible!
Ugh, my backpack's gone.
And my bus pass was in it.
Looks like we're walking home, Poc—
Oh no! Your key collar! It must've come off in the fight.
Dad's gonna ground me for*ever*.

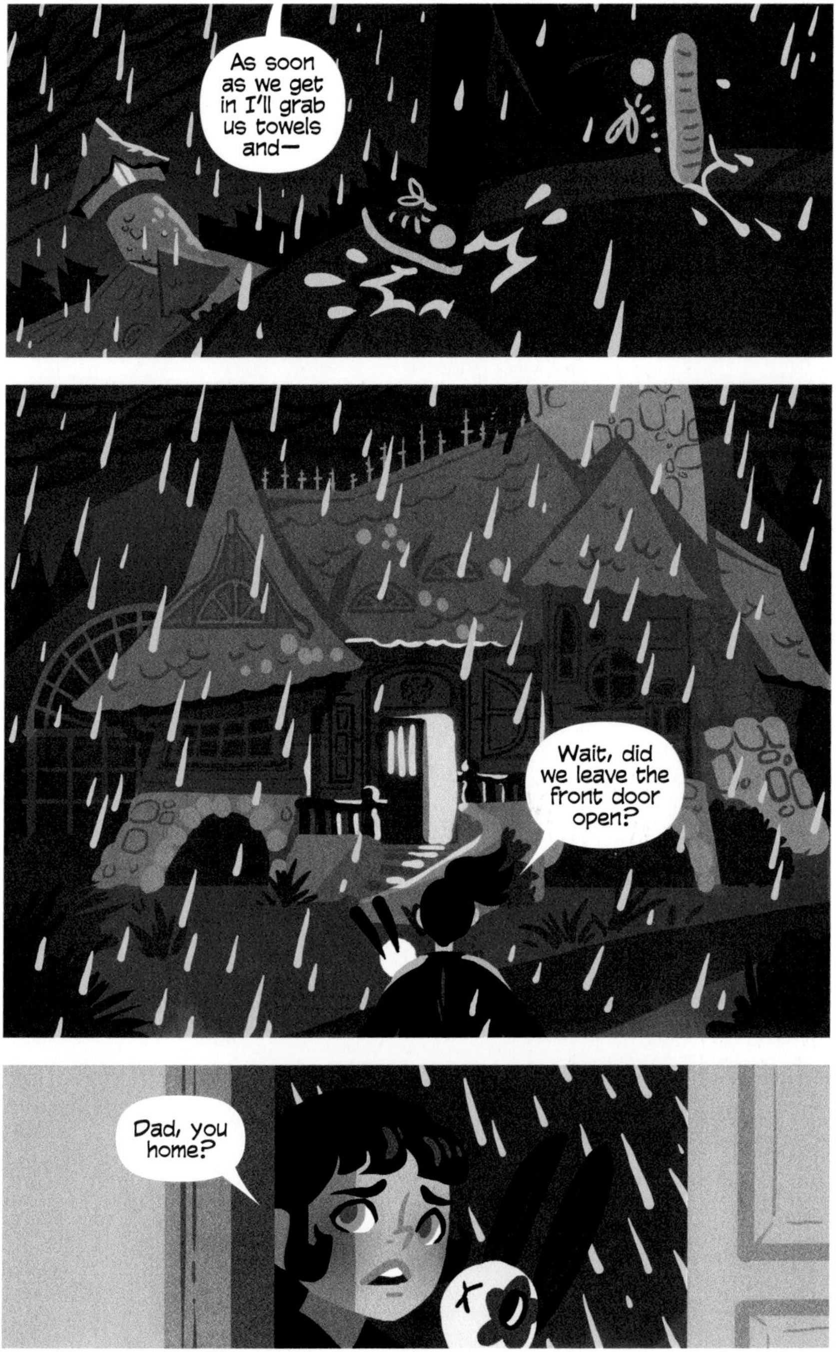
As soon as we get in I'll grab us towels and—
Wait, did we leave the front door open?
Dad, you home?

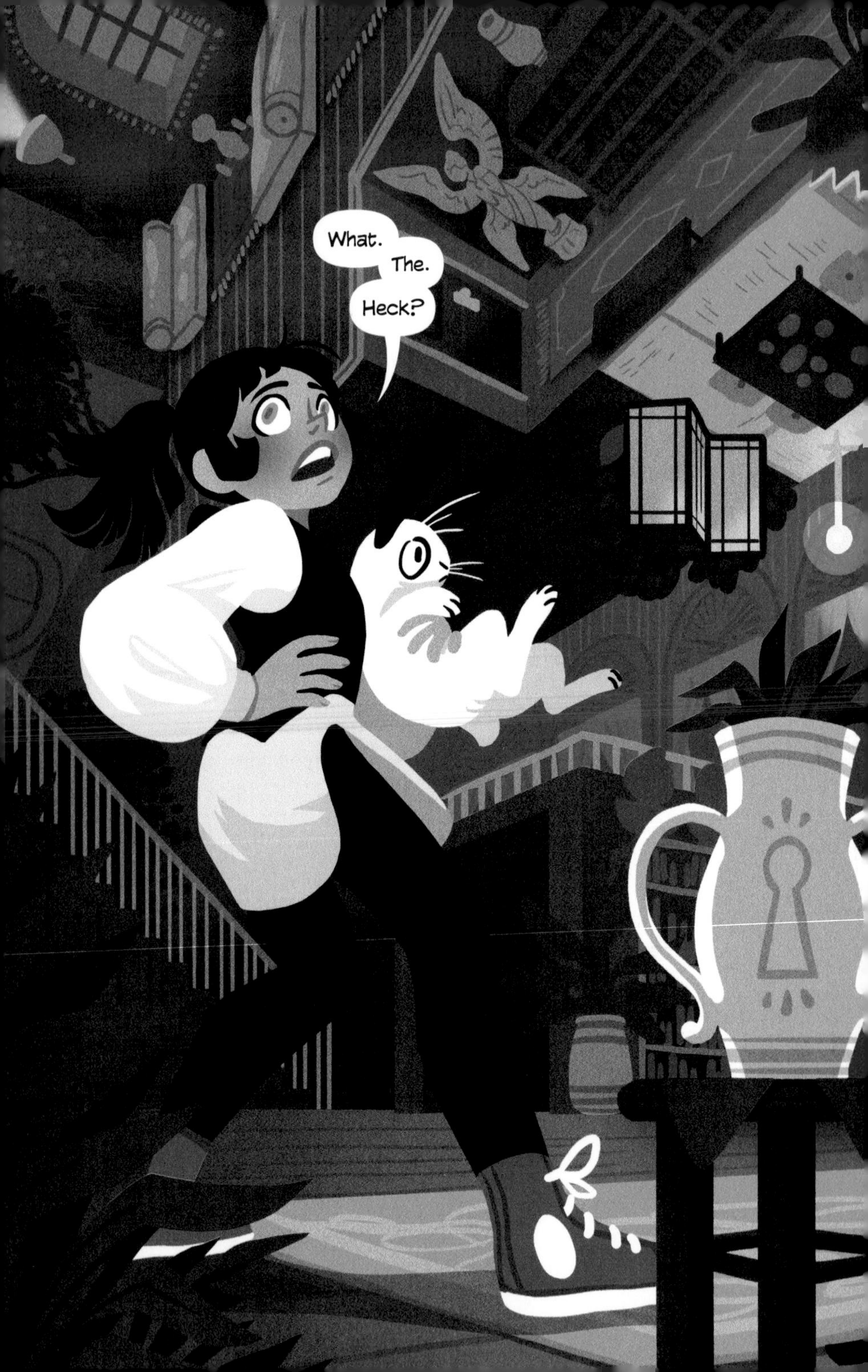
What.
The.
Heck?

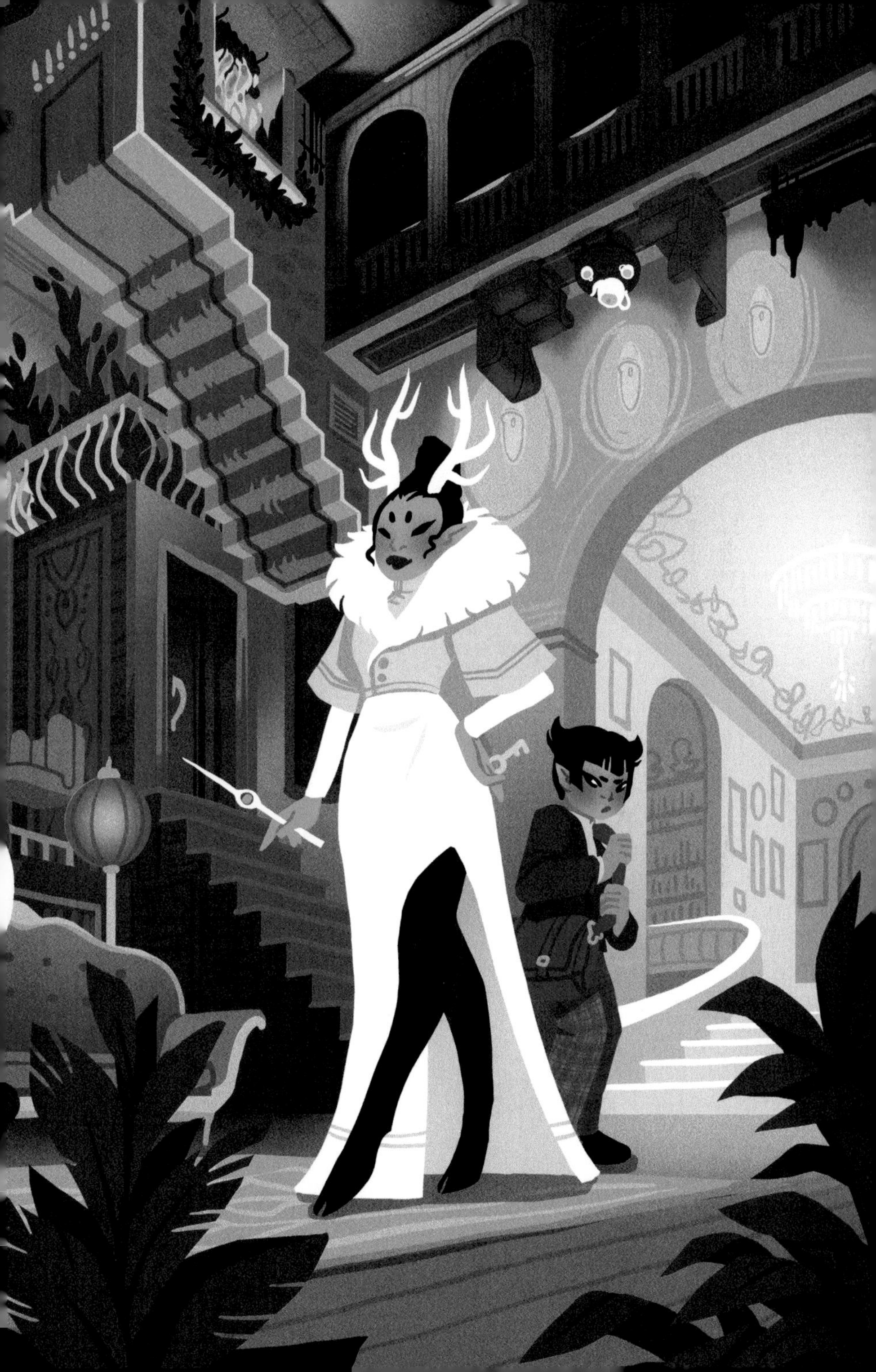

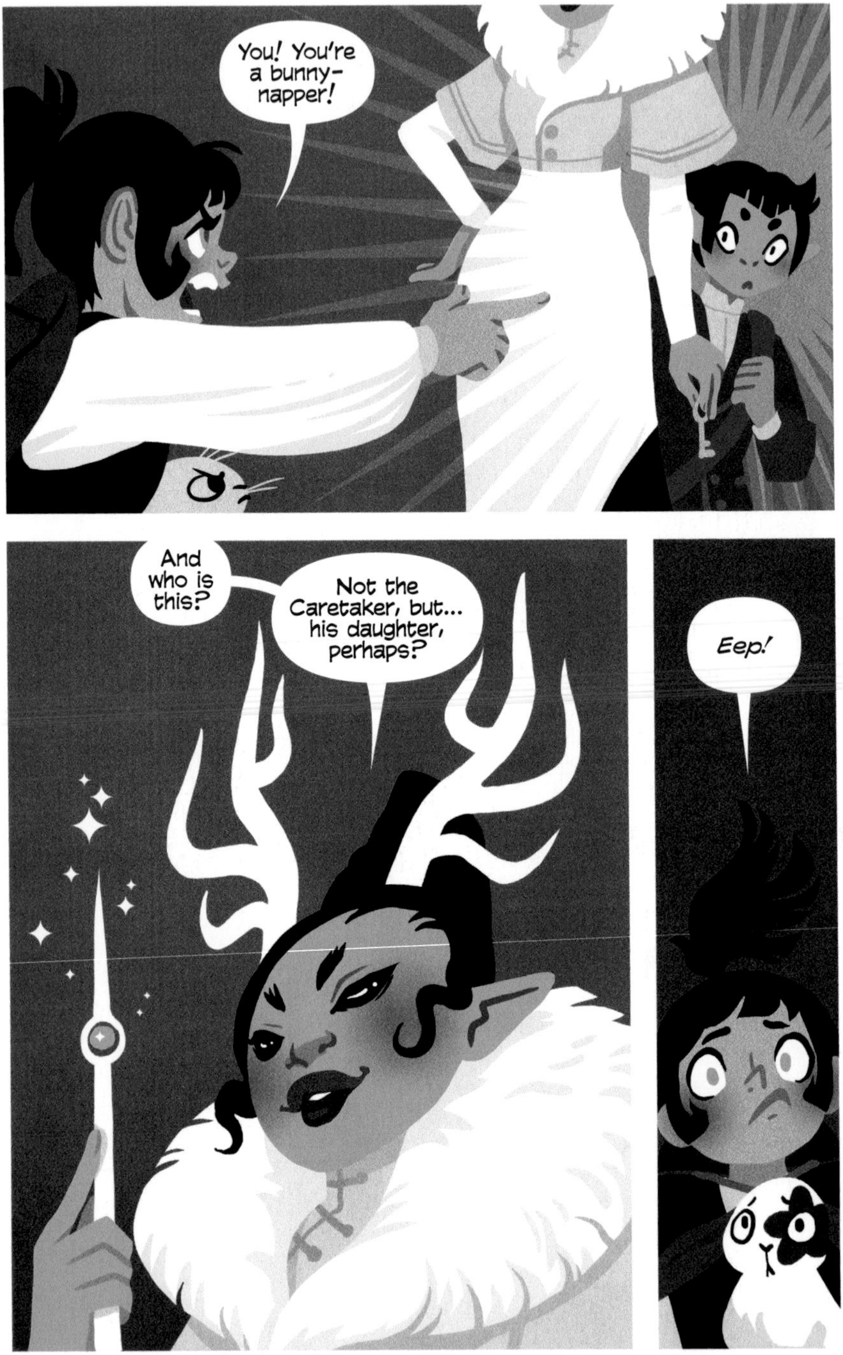
You! You're a bunny-napper!
And who is this?
Not the Caretaker, but... his daughter, perhaps?
Eep!

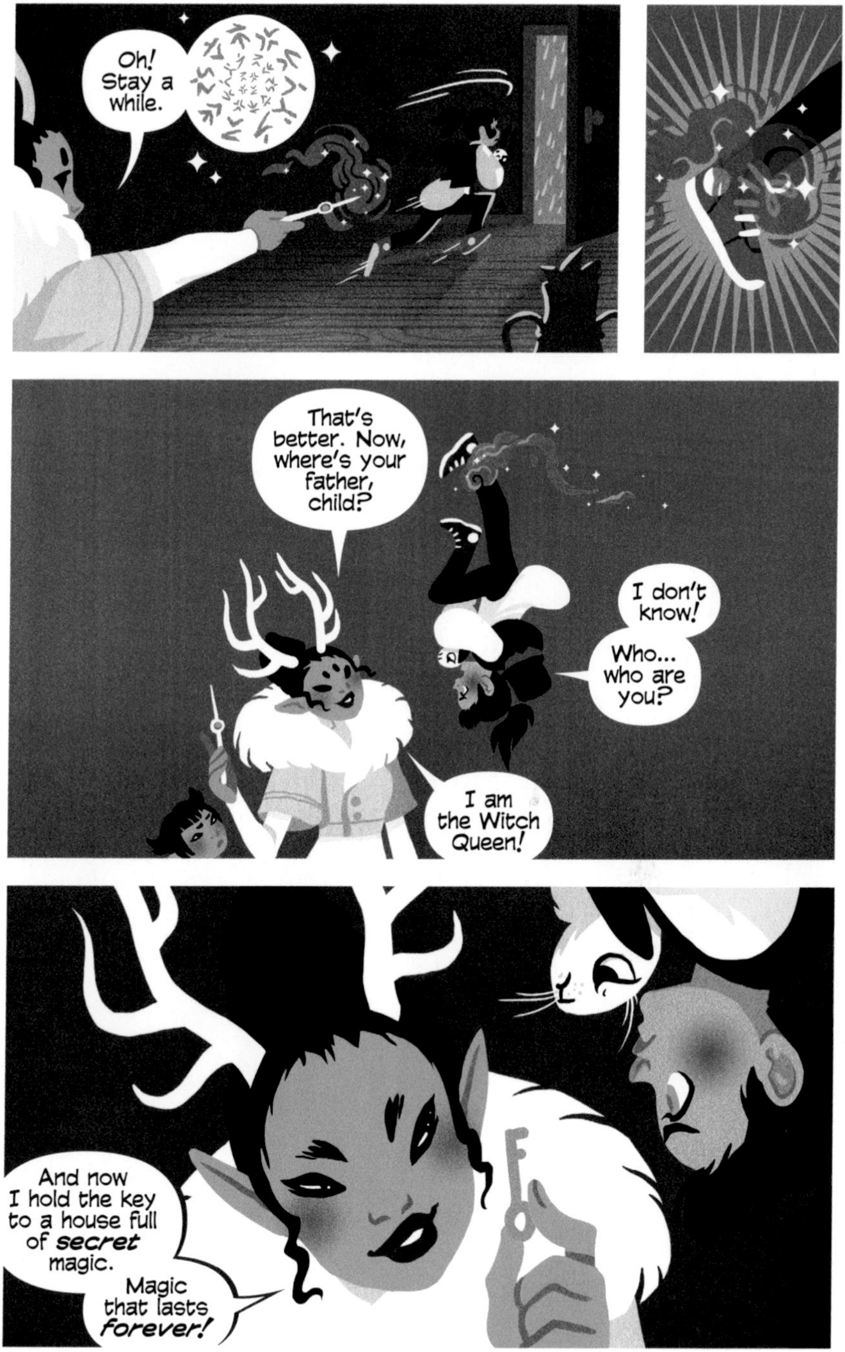
Oh! Stay a while.
That's better. Now, where's your father, child?
I don't know!
Who... who are you?
I am the Witch Queen!
And now I hold the key to a house full of secret magic.
Magic that lasts forever!

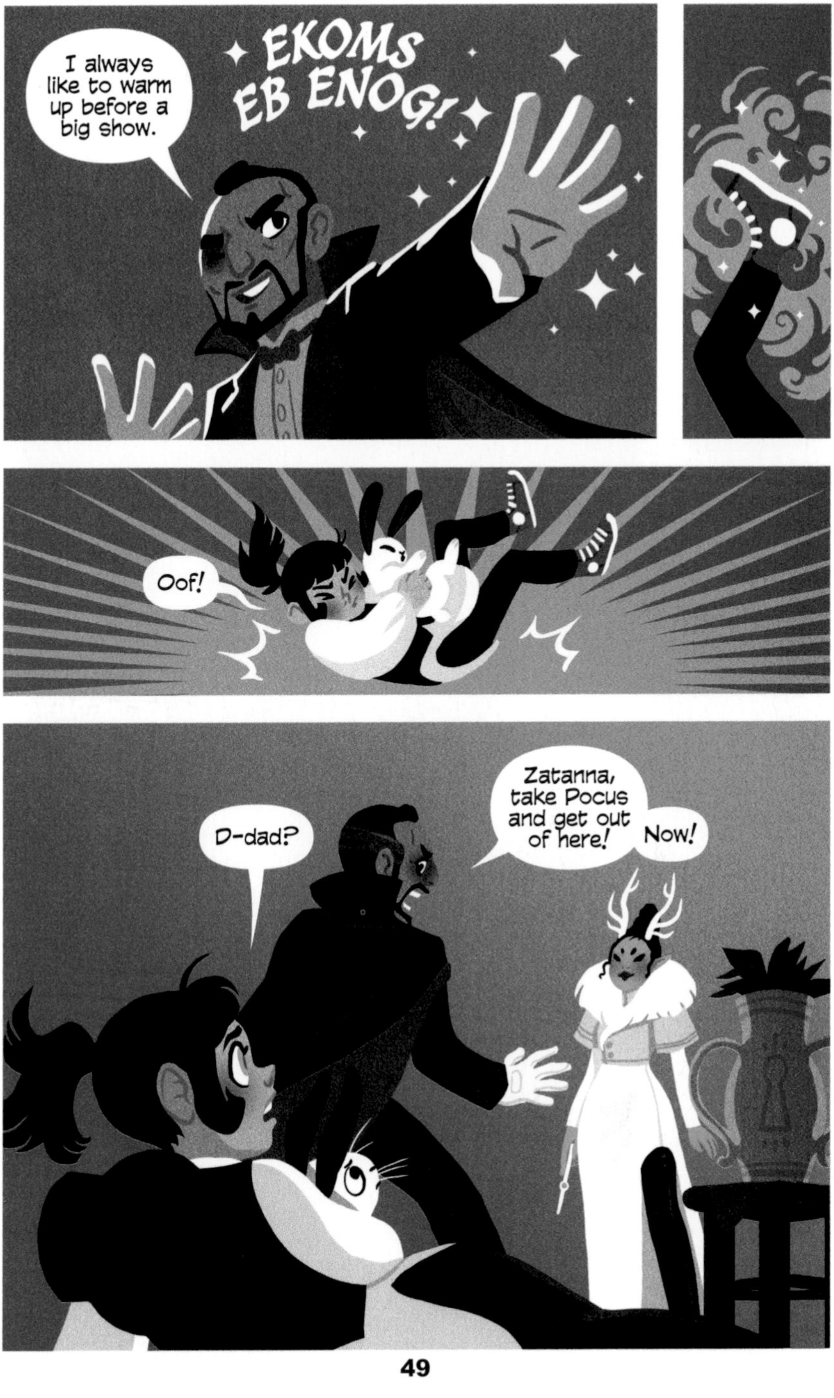
I always like to warm up before a big show.
EKOMS EB ENOG!
Oof!
D-dad?
Zatanna, take Pocus and get out of here!
Now!

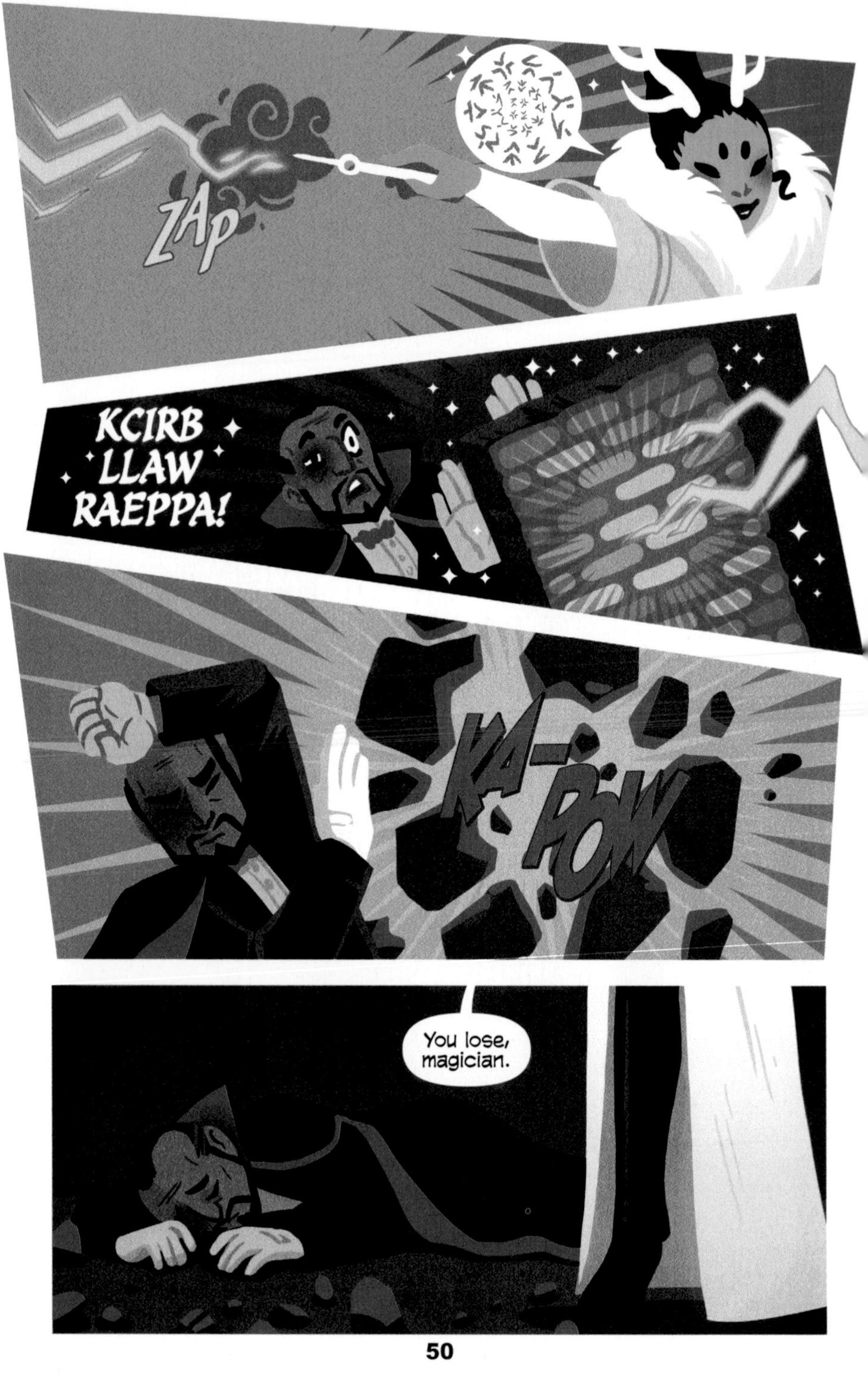
ZAP
KCIRB LLAW RAEPPA!
KA-POW
You lose, magician.

52

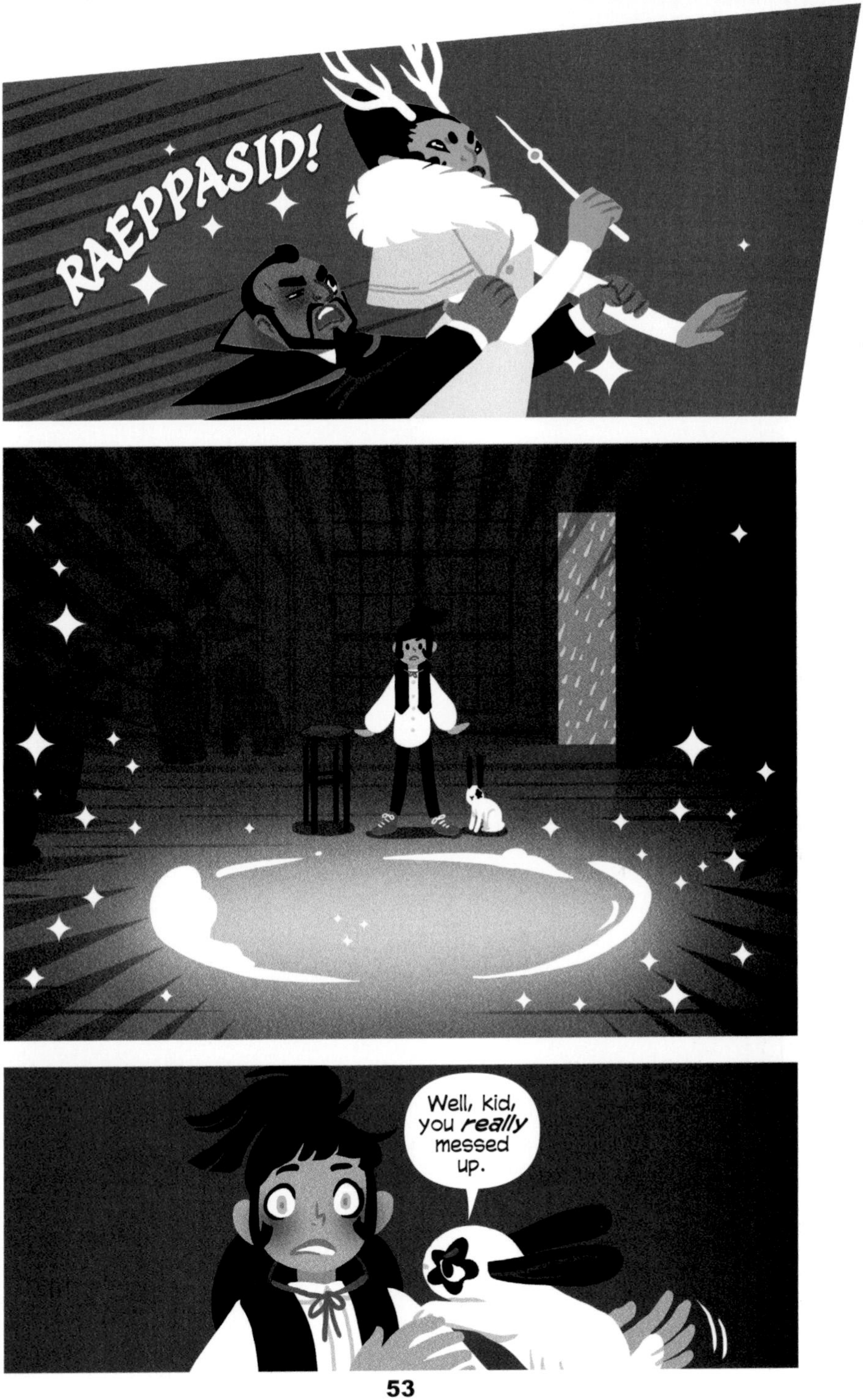
RAEPPASID!
Well, kid, you really messed up.

Chapter Three

56

57

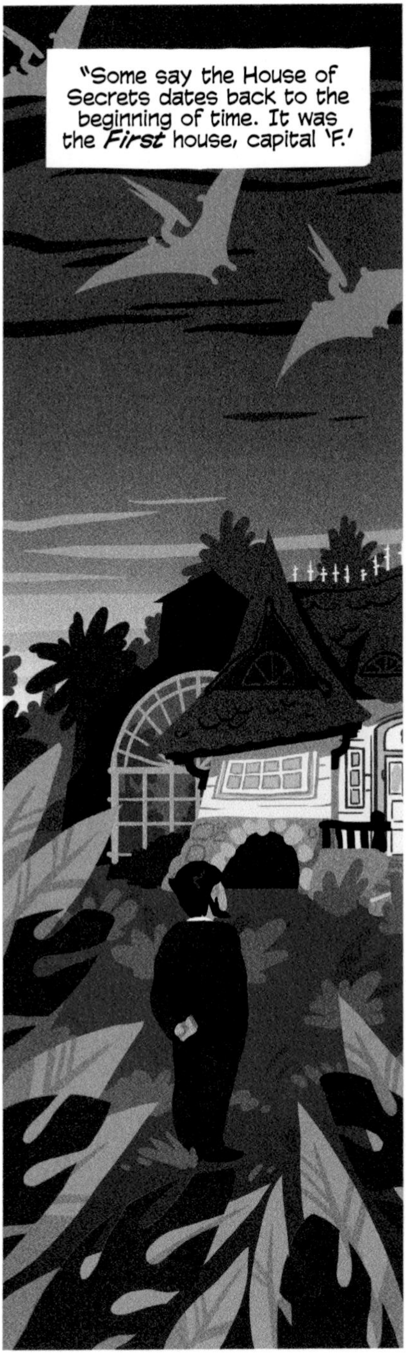
"Some say the House of Secrets dates back to the beginning of time. It was the *First* house, capital 'F.'

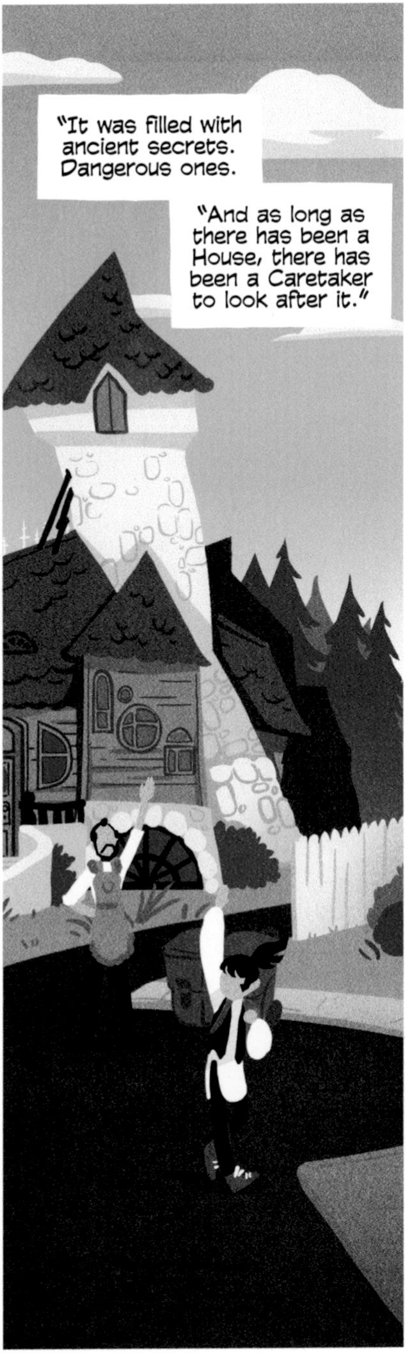
"It was filled with ancient secrets. Dangerous ones.
"And as long as there has been a House, there has been a Caretaker to look after it."

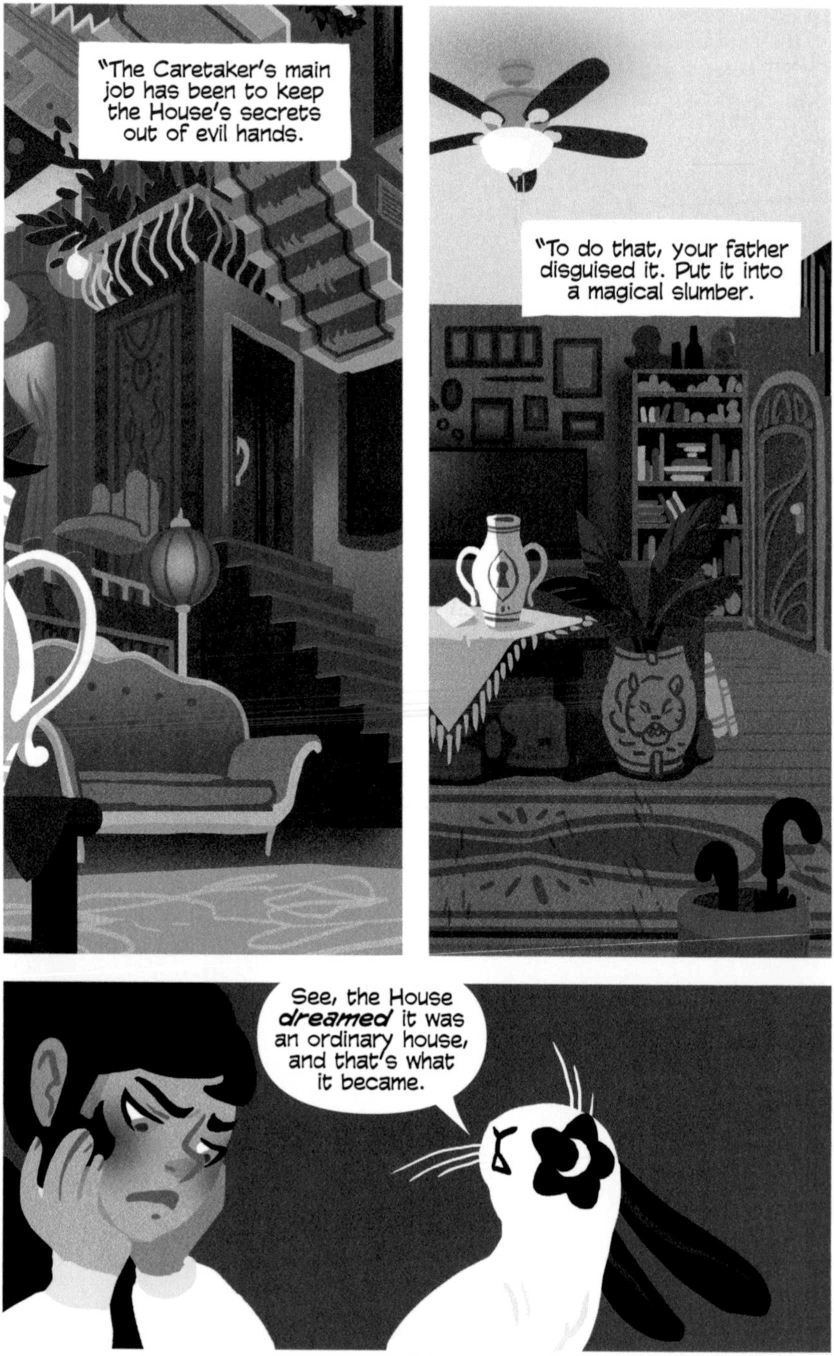
"The Caretaker's main job has been to keep the House's secrets out of evil hands.
"To do that, your father disguised it. Put it into a magical slumber.
See, the House *dreamed* it was an ordinary house, and that's what it became.

61

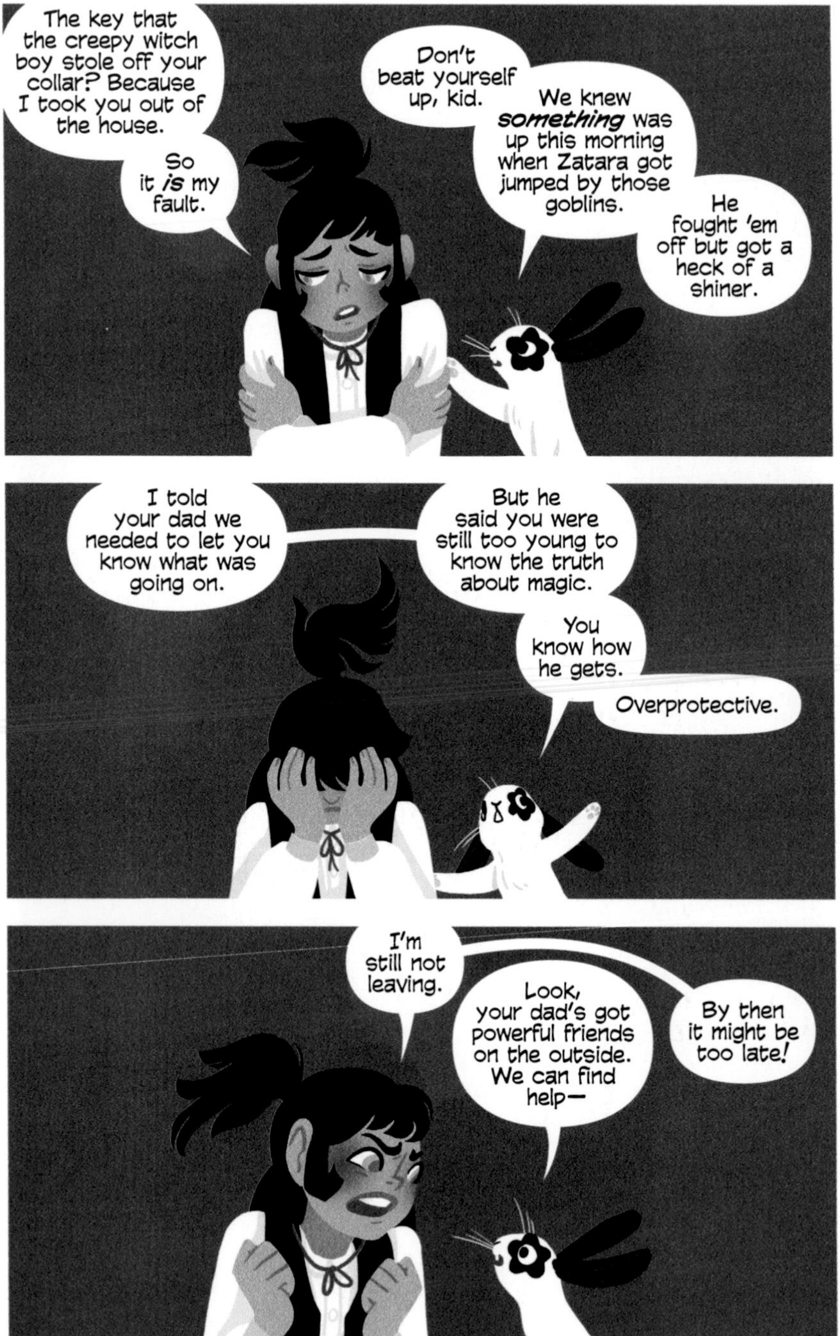
The key that the creepy witch boy stole off your collar? Because I took you out of the house.
So it *is* my fault.
Don't beat yourself up, kid.
We knew ***something*** was up this morning when Zatara got jumped by those goblins.
He fought 'em off but got a heck of a shiner.
I told your dad we needed to let you know what was going on.
But he said you were still too young to know the truth about magic.
You know how he gets.
Overprotective.
I'm still not leaving.
Look, your dad's got powerful friends on the outside. We can find help—
By then it might be too late!

63

64

70

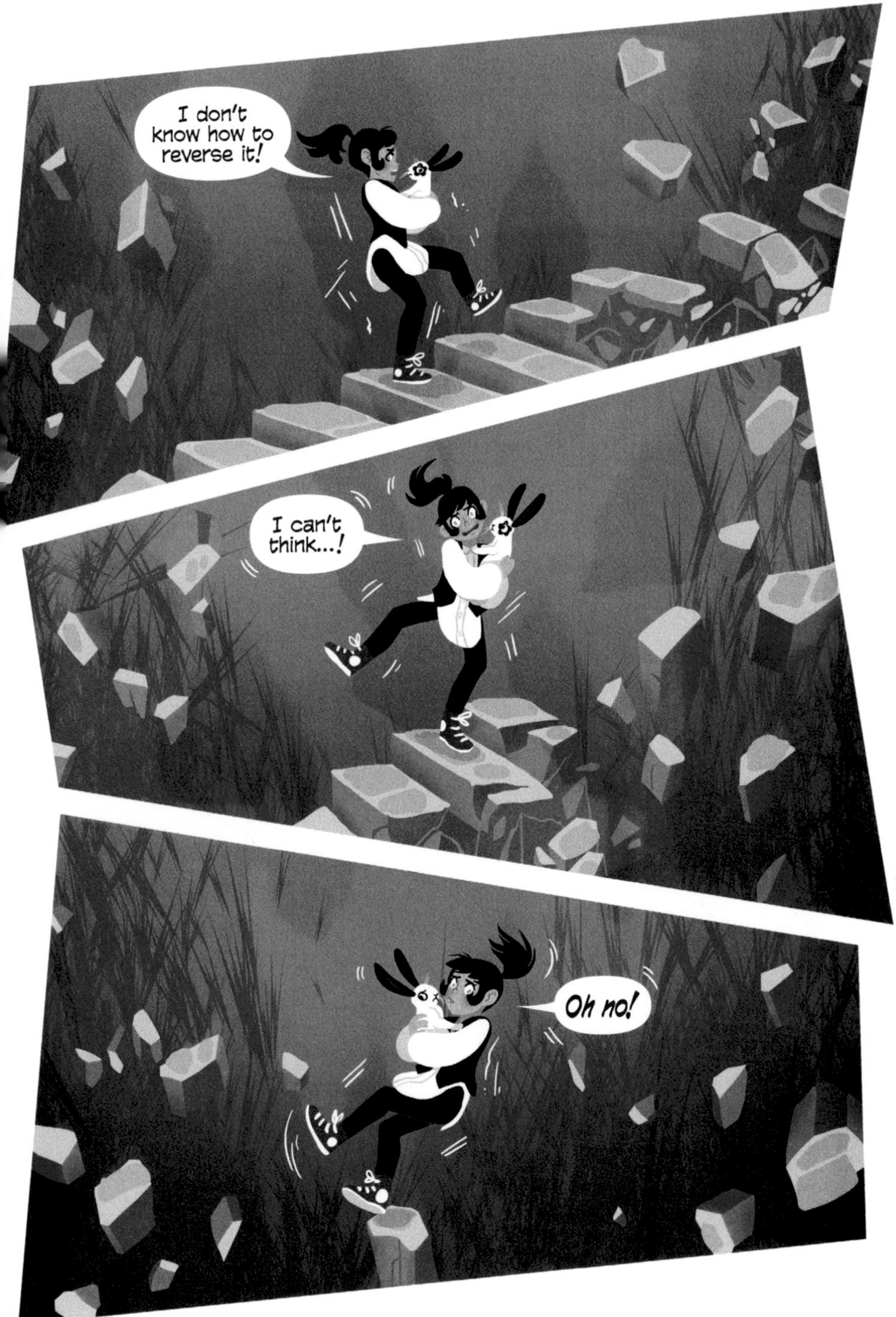
I don't know how to reverse it!
I can't think...!
Oh no!

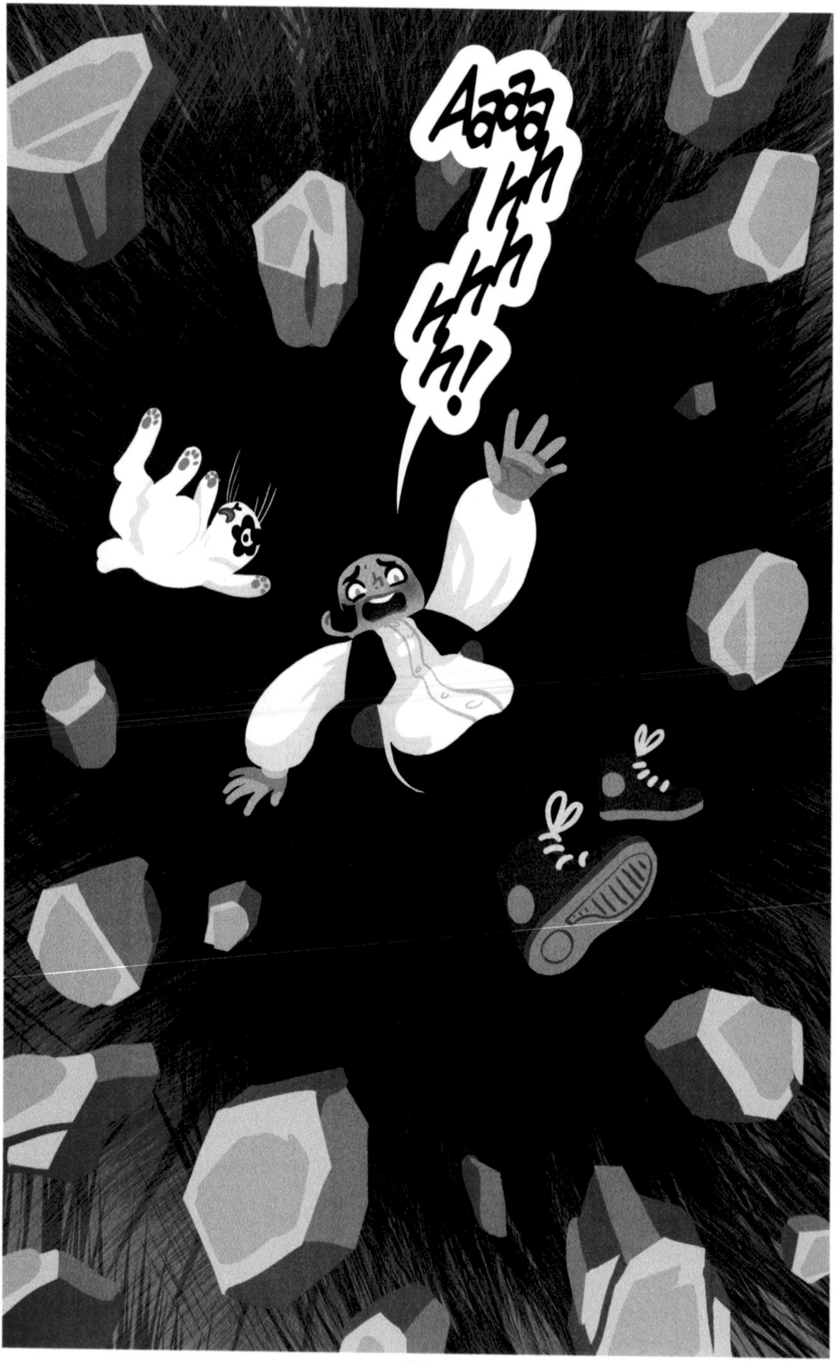
Aaaahhhhhh!

Chapter Four

74

75

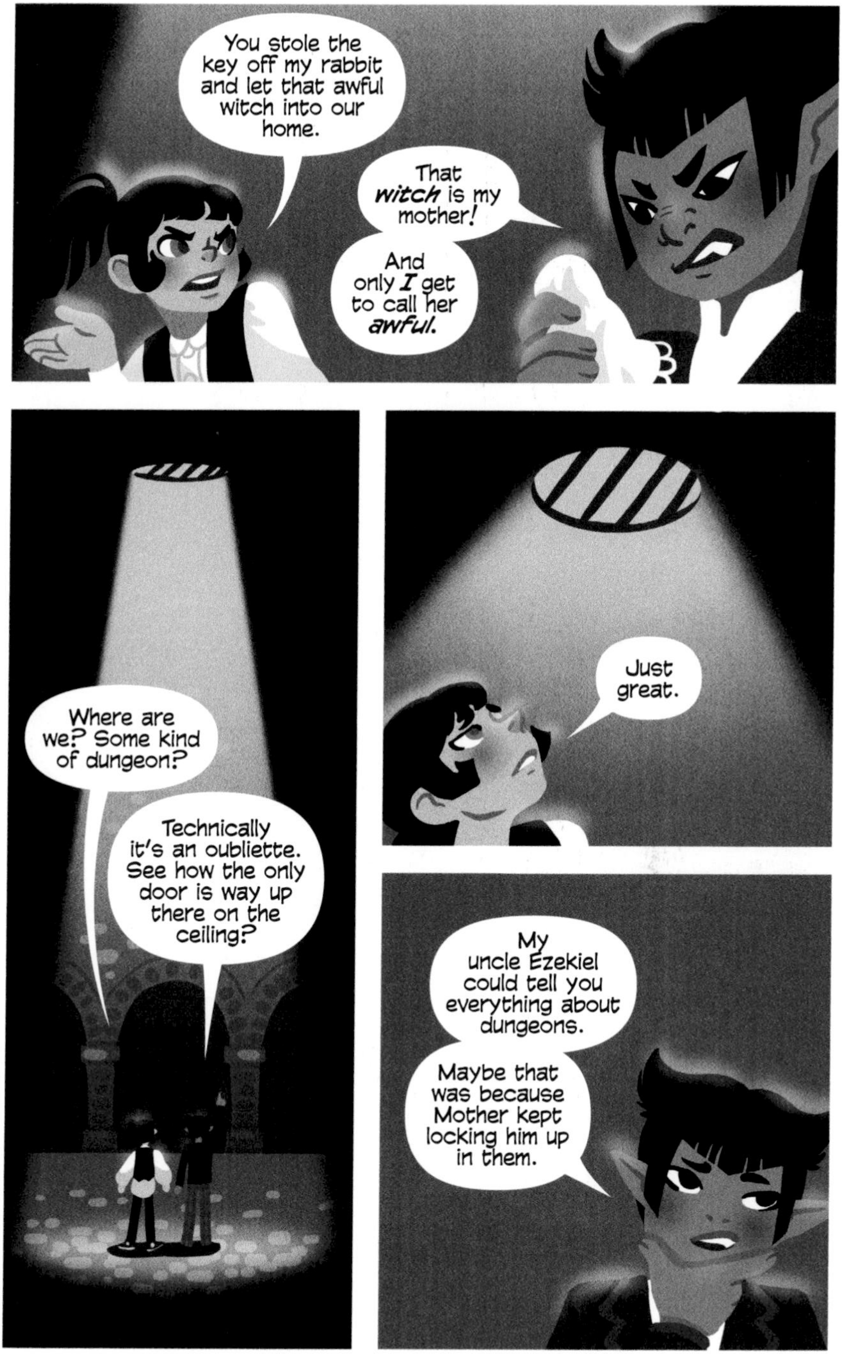
You stole the key off my rabbit and let that awful witch into our home.
That *witch* is my mother!
And only *I* get to call her *awful.*
Where are we? Some kind of dungeon?
Technically it's an oubliette. See how the only door is way up there on the ceiling?
Just great.
My uncle Ezekiel could tell you everything about dungeons.
Maybe that was because Mother kept locking him up in them.

78

79

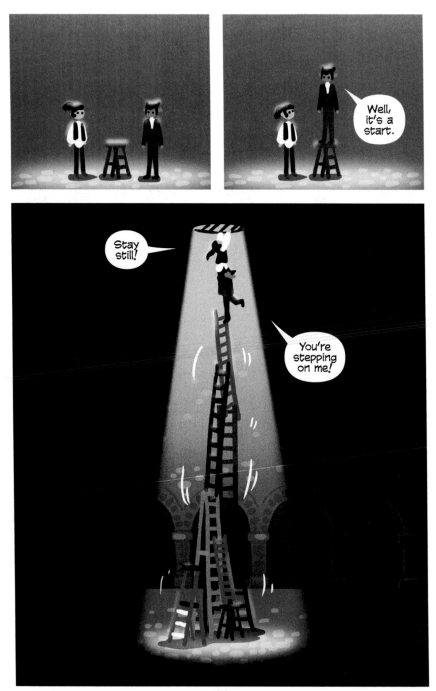

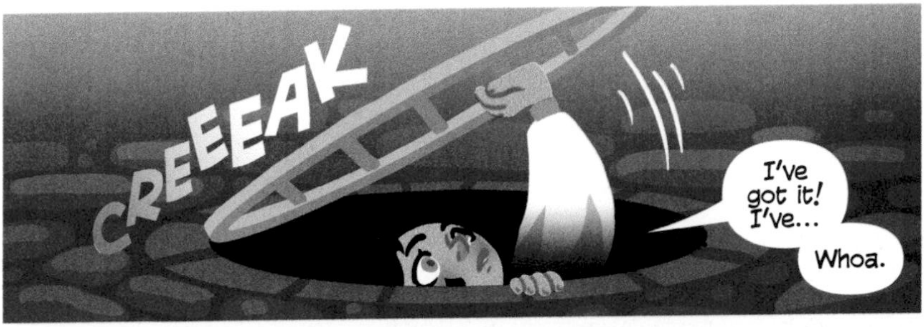
CREEEAK
I've got it! I've...
Whoa.

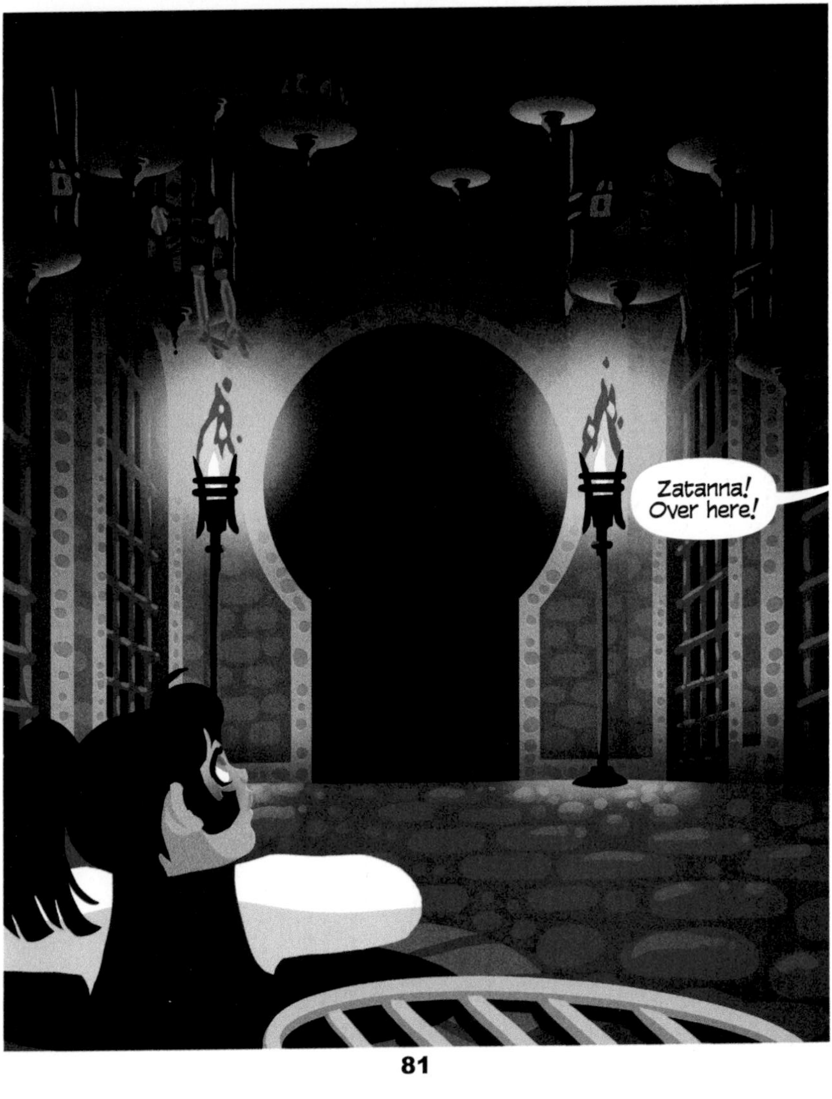
Zatanna! Over here!

83

84

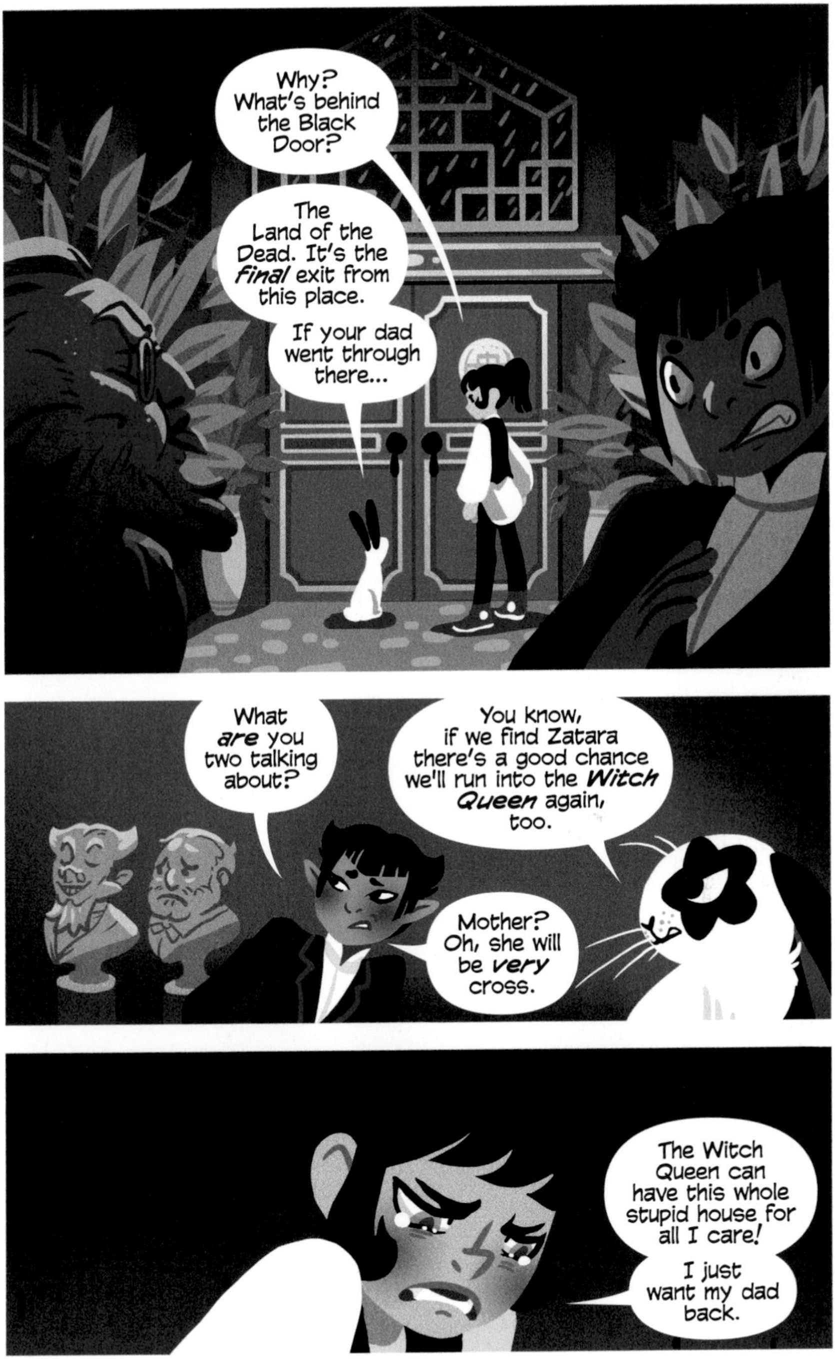
Why? What's behind the Black Door?
The Land of the Dead. It's the *final* exit from this place.
If your dad went through there...
What *are* you two talking about?
You know, if we find Zatara there's a good chance we'll run into the *Witch Queen* again, too.
Mother? Oh, she will be *very* cross.
The Witch Queen can have this whole stupid house for all I care!
I just want my dad back.

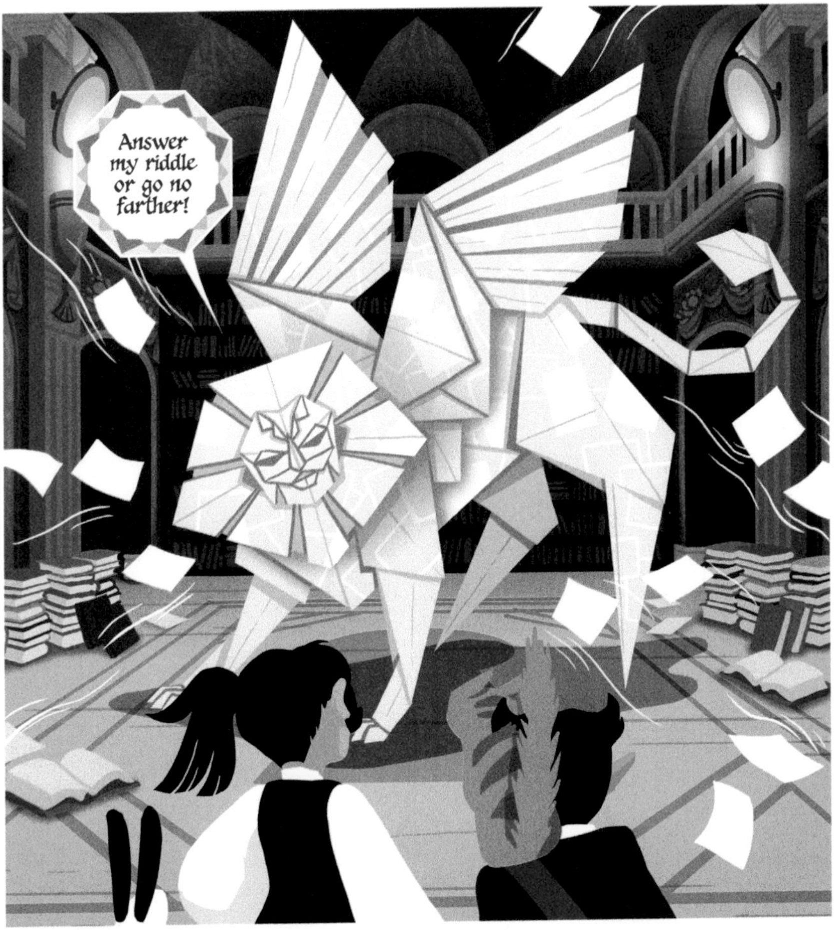
Answer my riddle or go no farther!

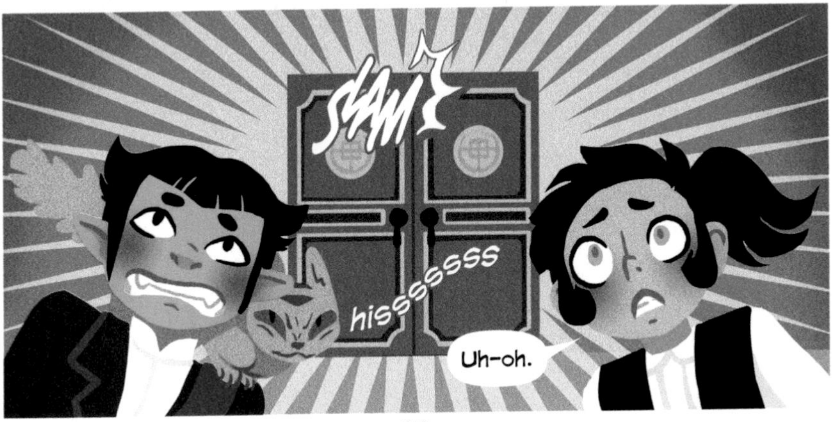
SLAM!
hissssssss
Uh-oh.

91

92

94

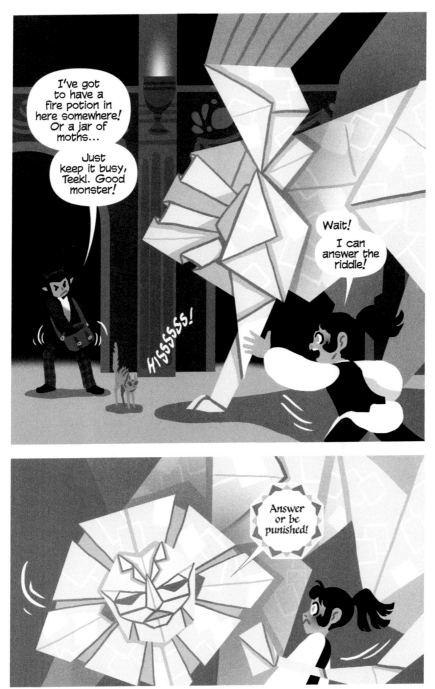

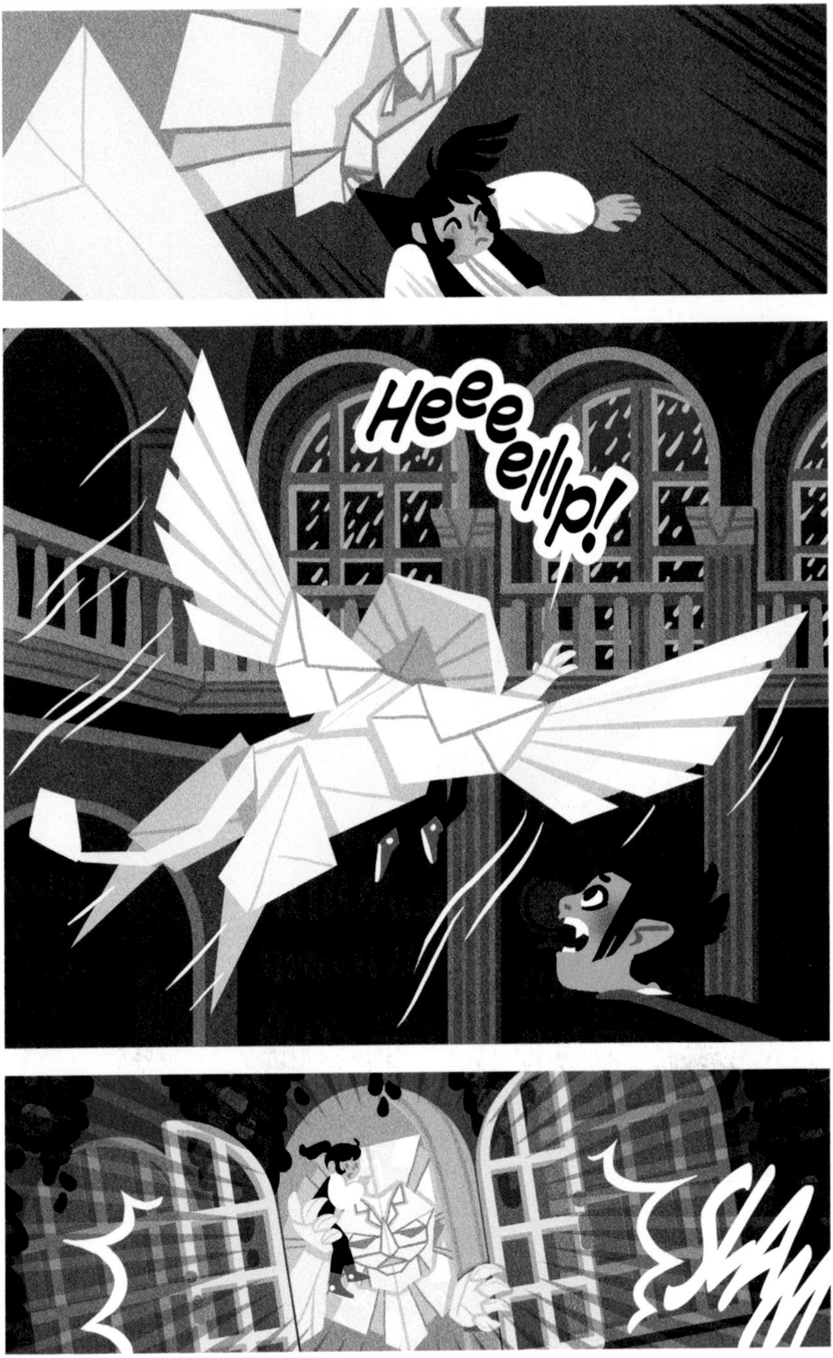
Heeeellp!
SLAM

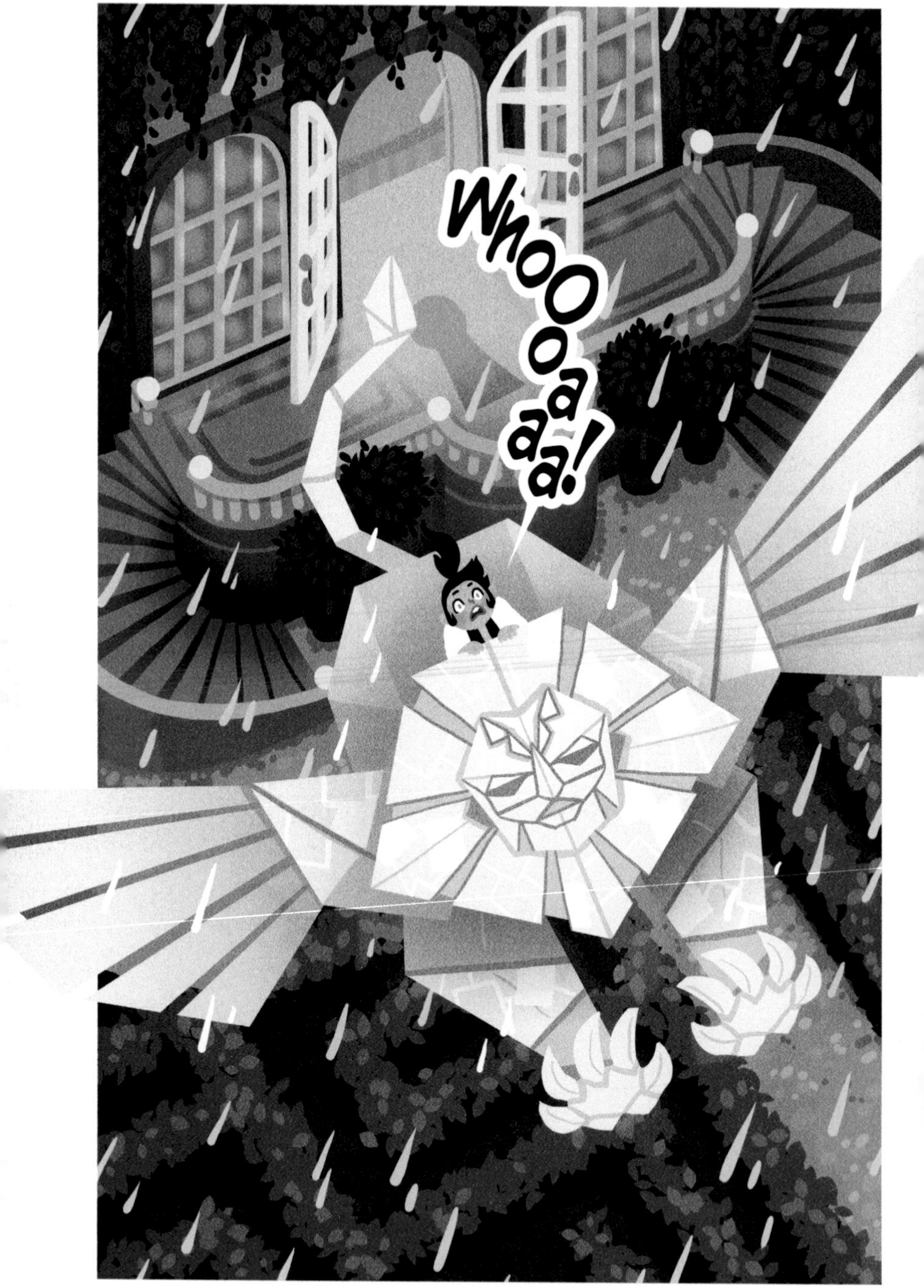
WhoOOoaaaa!

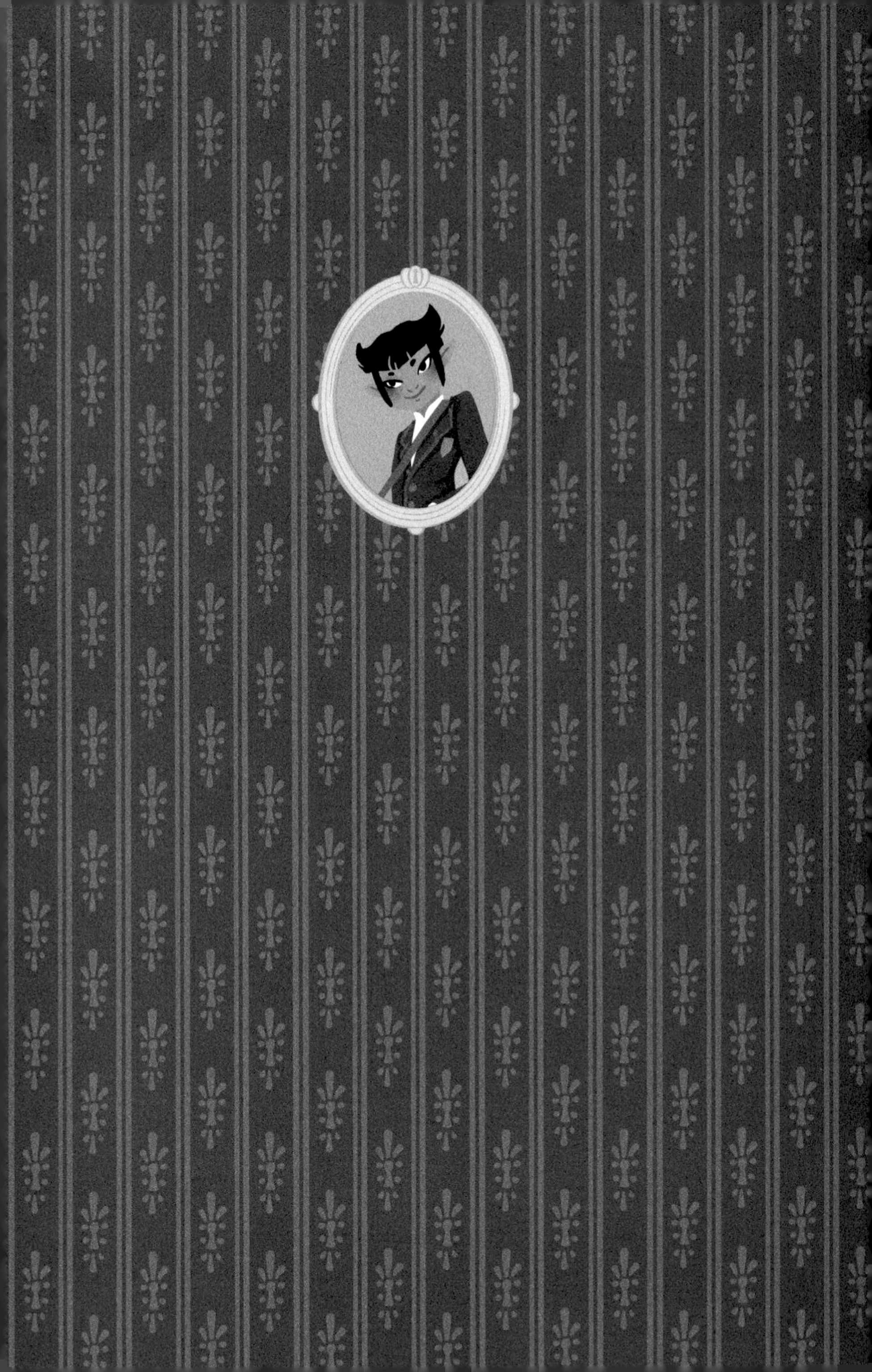

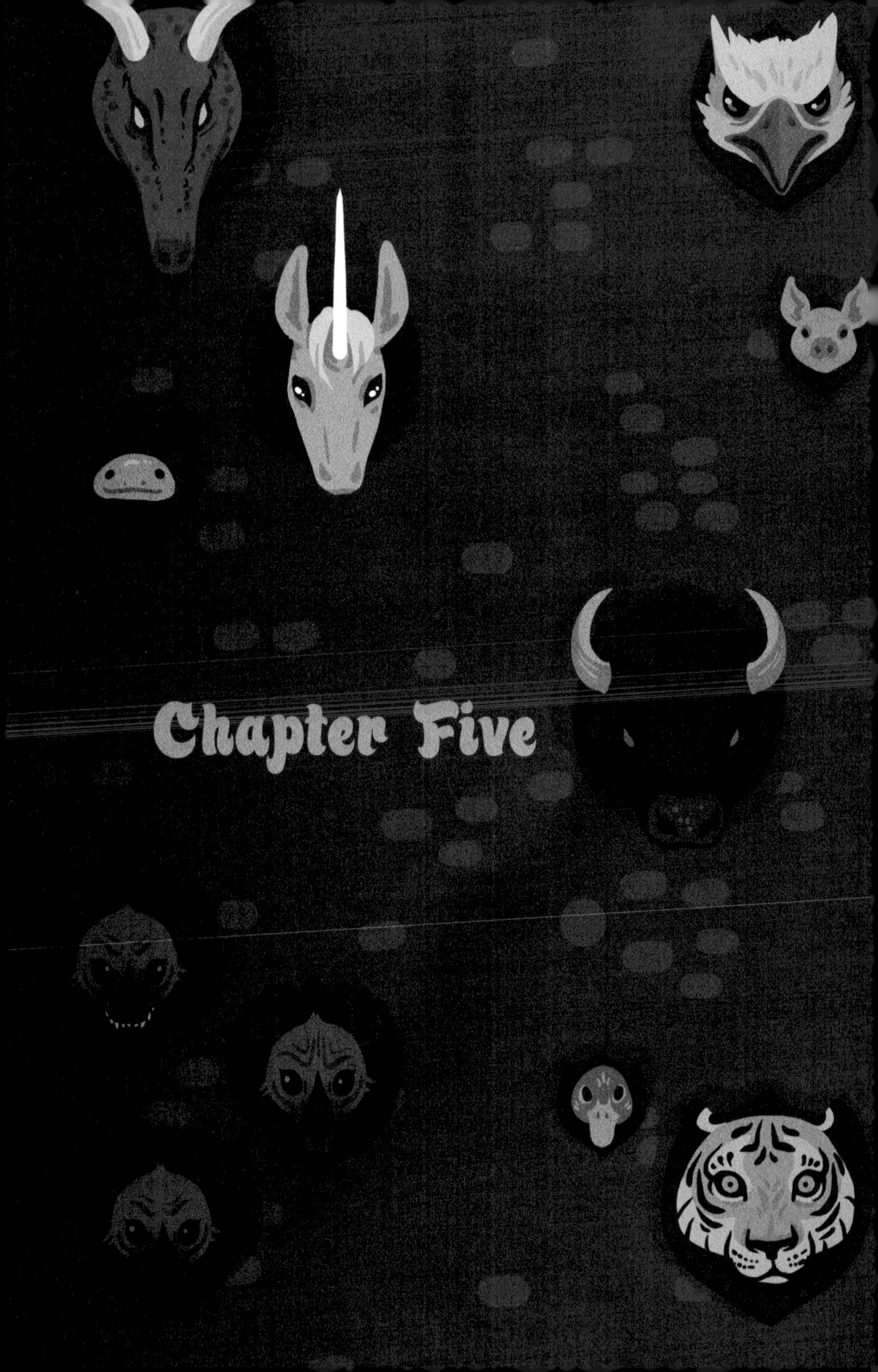

Chapter Five

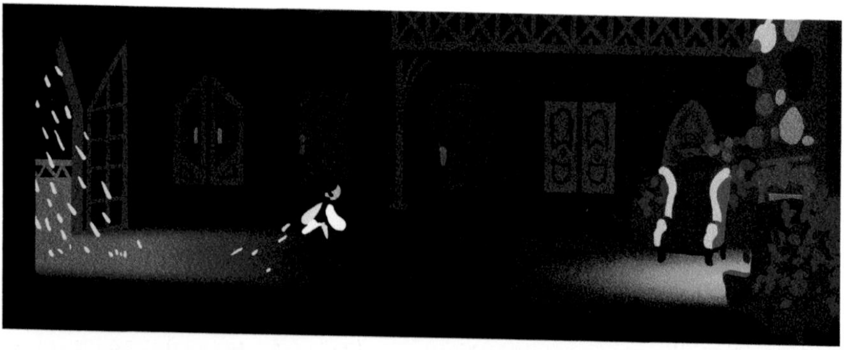

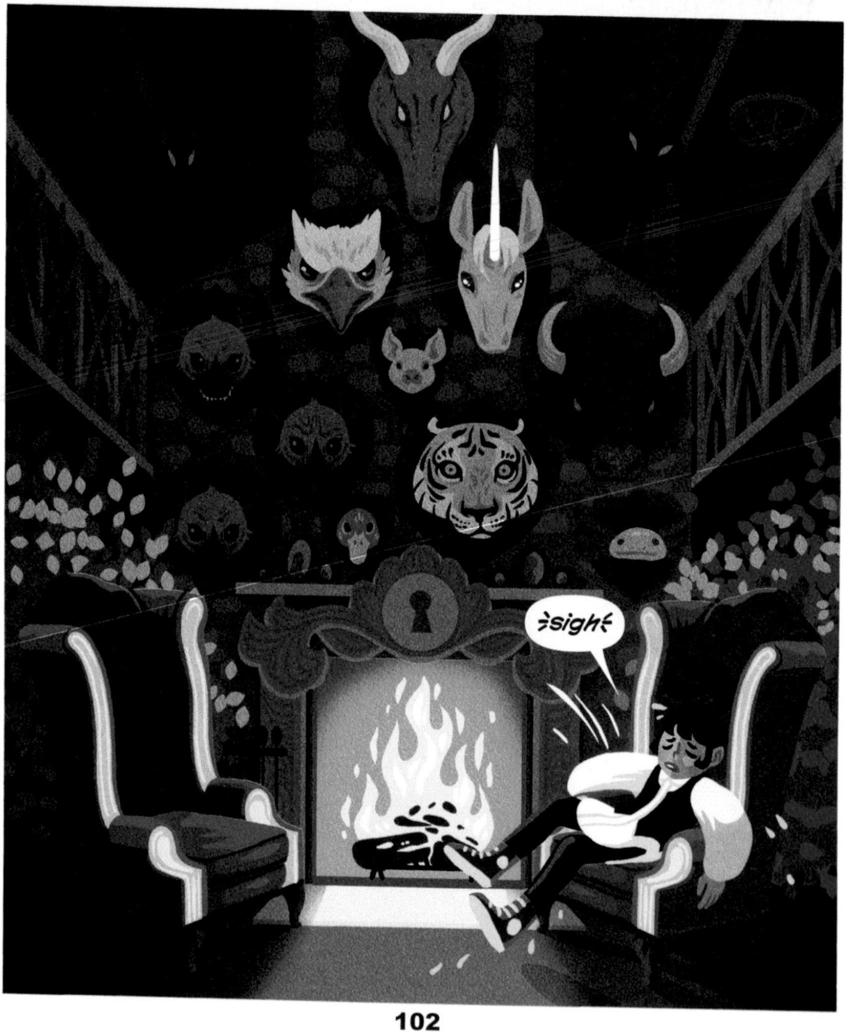
sigh

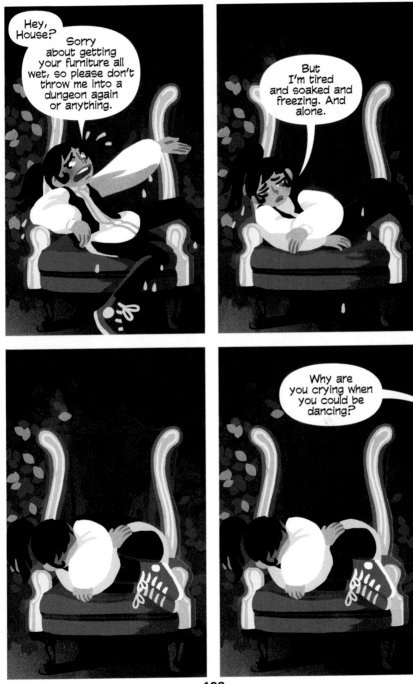

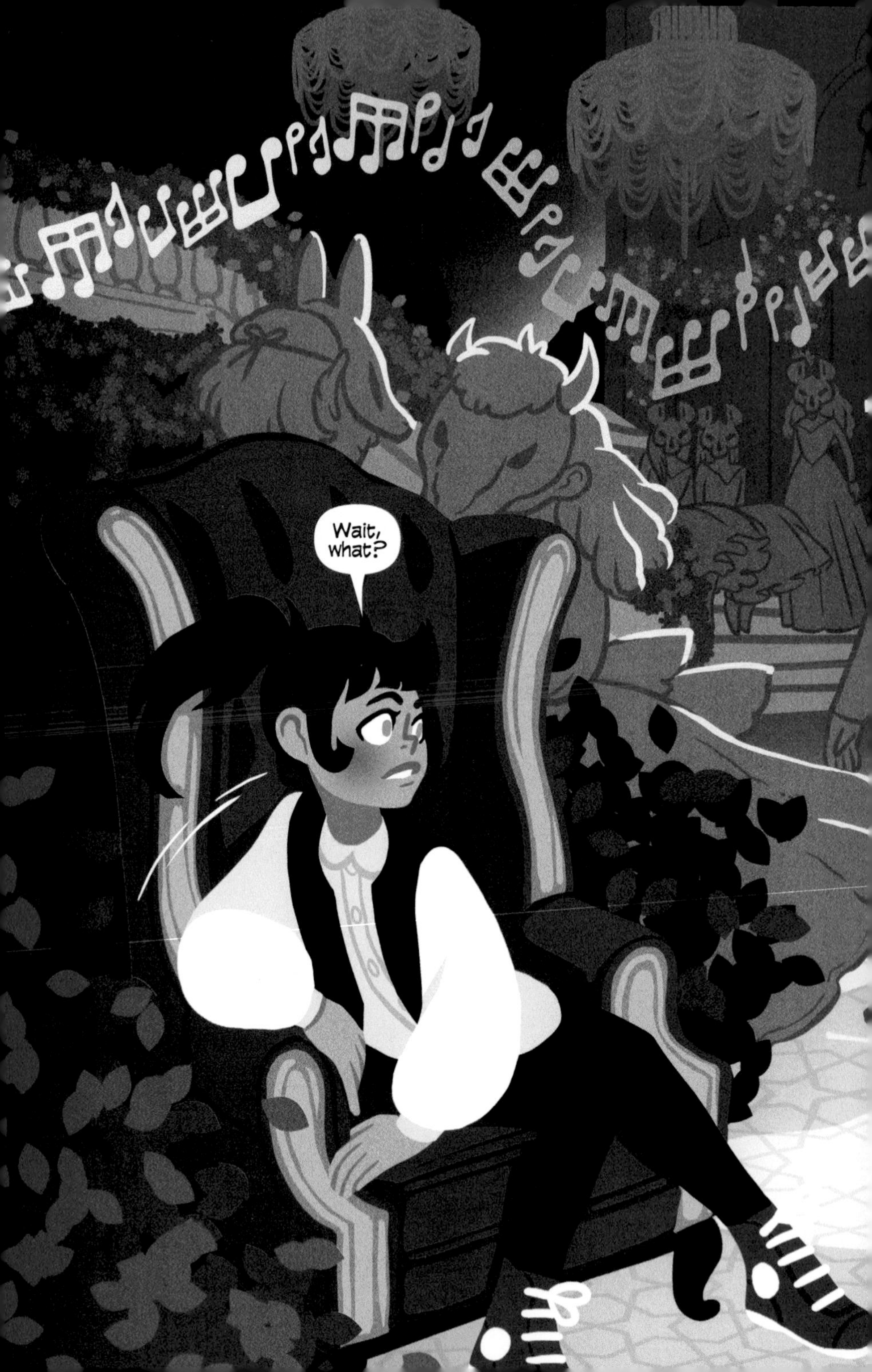
Wait, what?

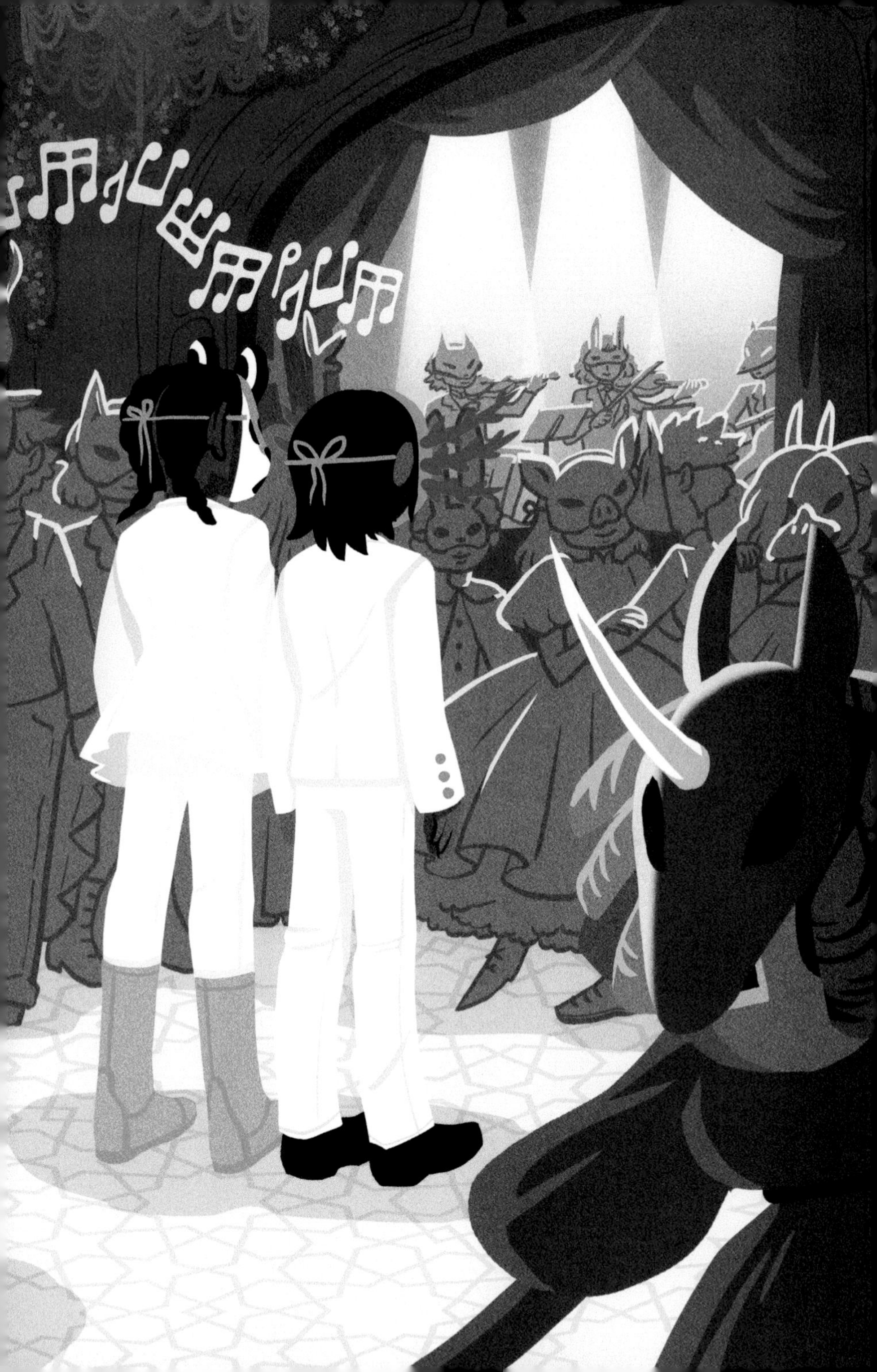

109

112

113

118

119

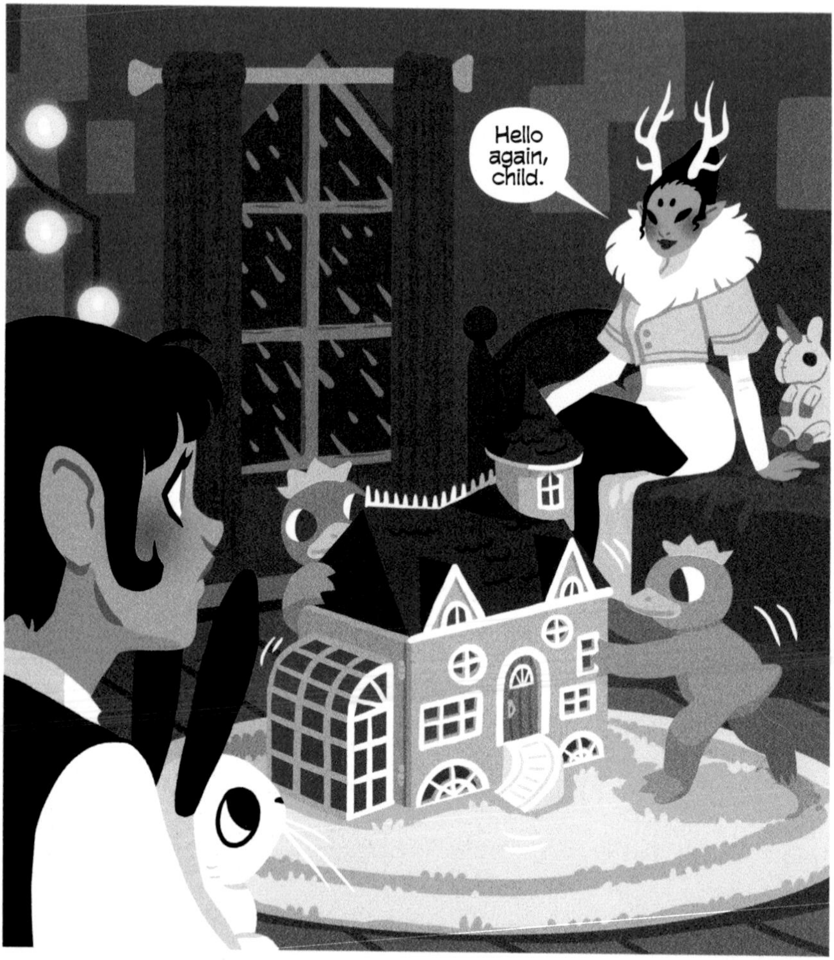
Hello again, child.

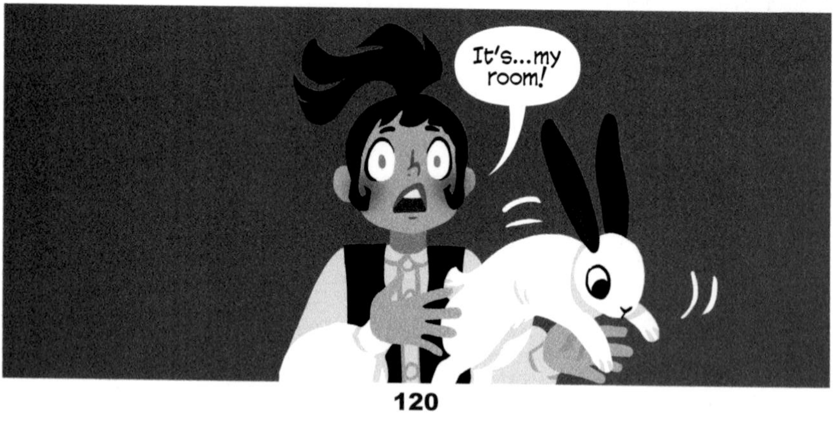
It's...my room!

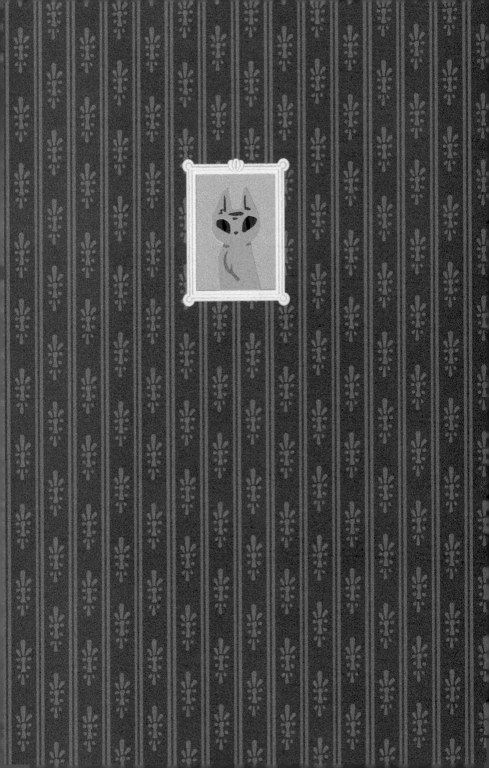

Chapter Six

123

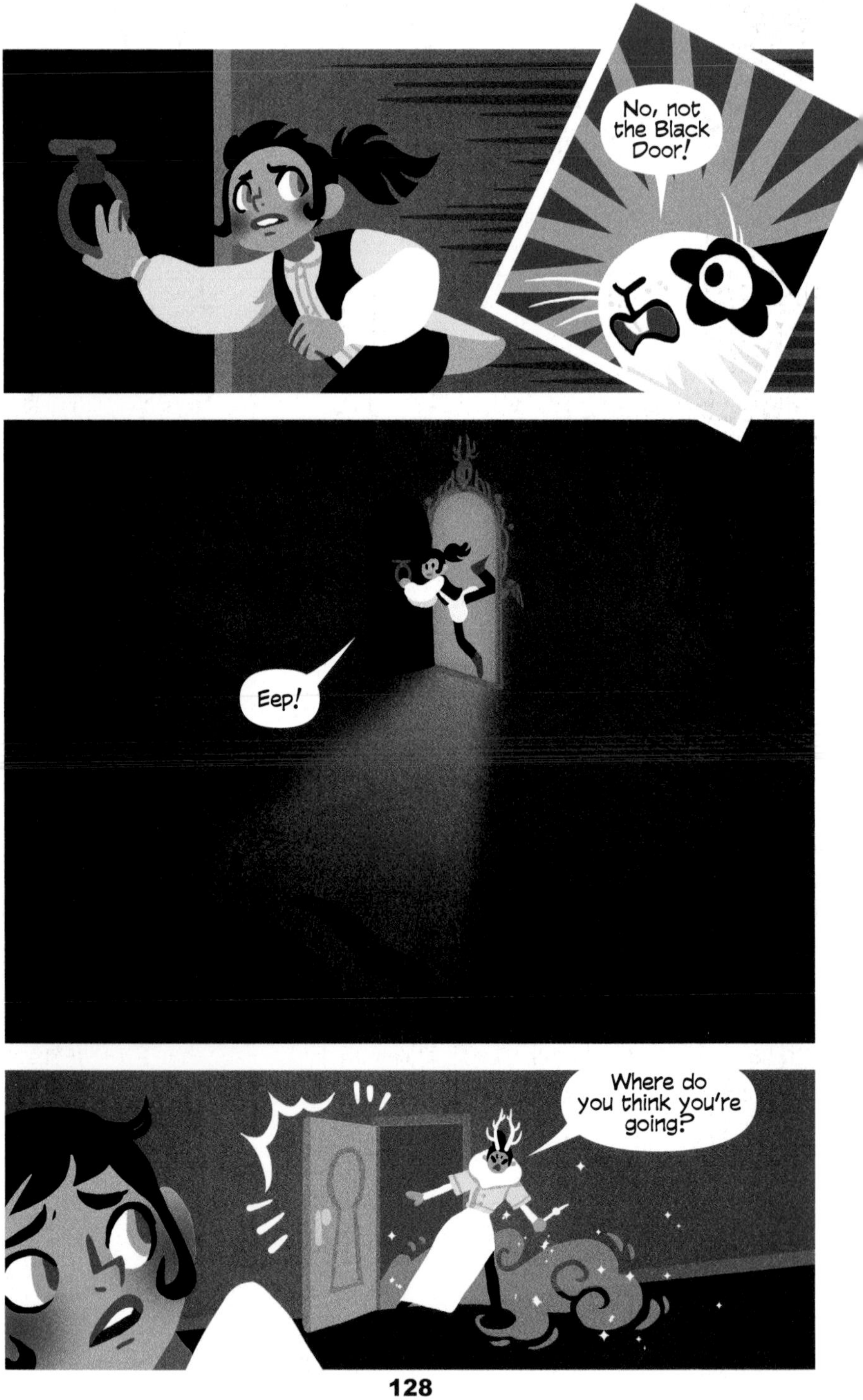
No, not the Black Door!
Eep!
Where do you think you're going?

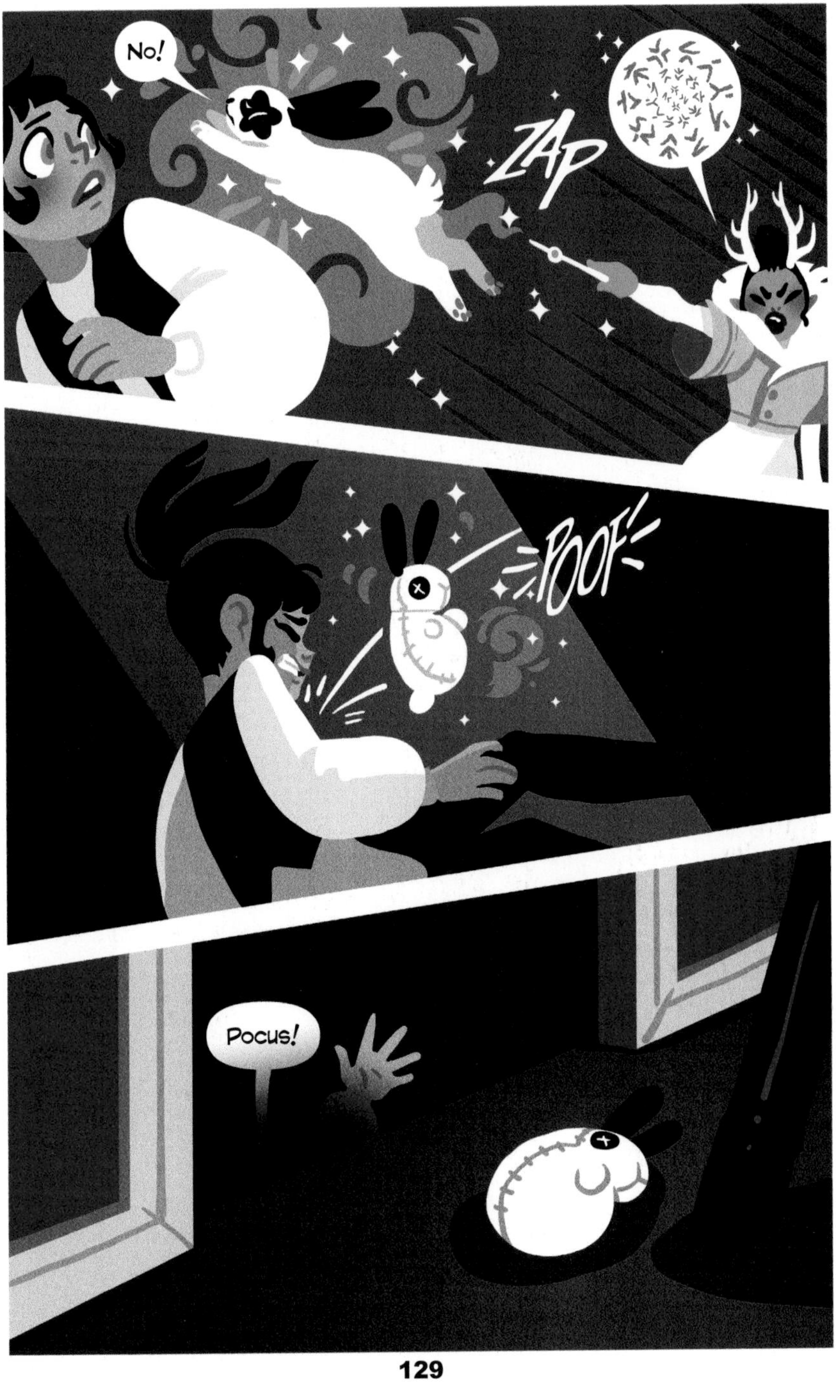
No!
ZAP
POOF
Pocus!

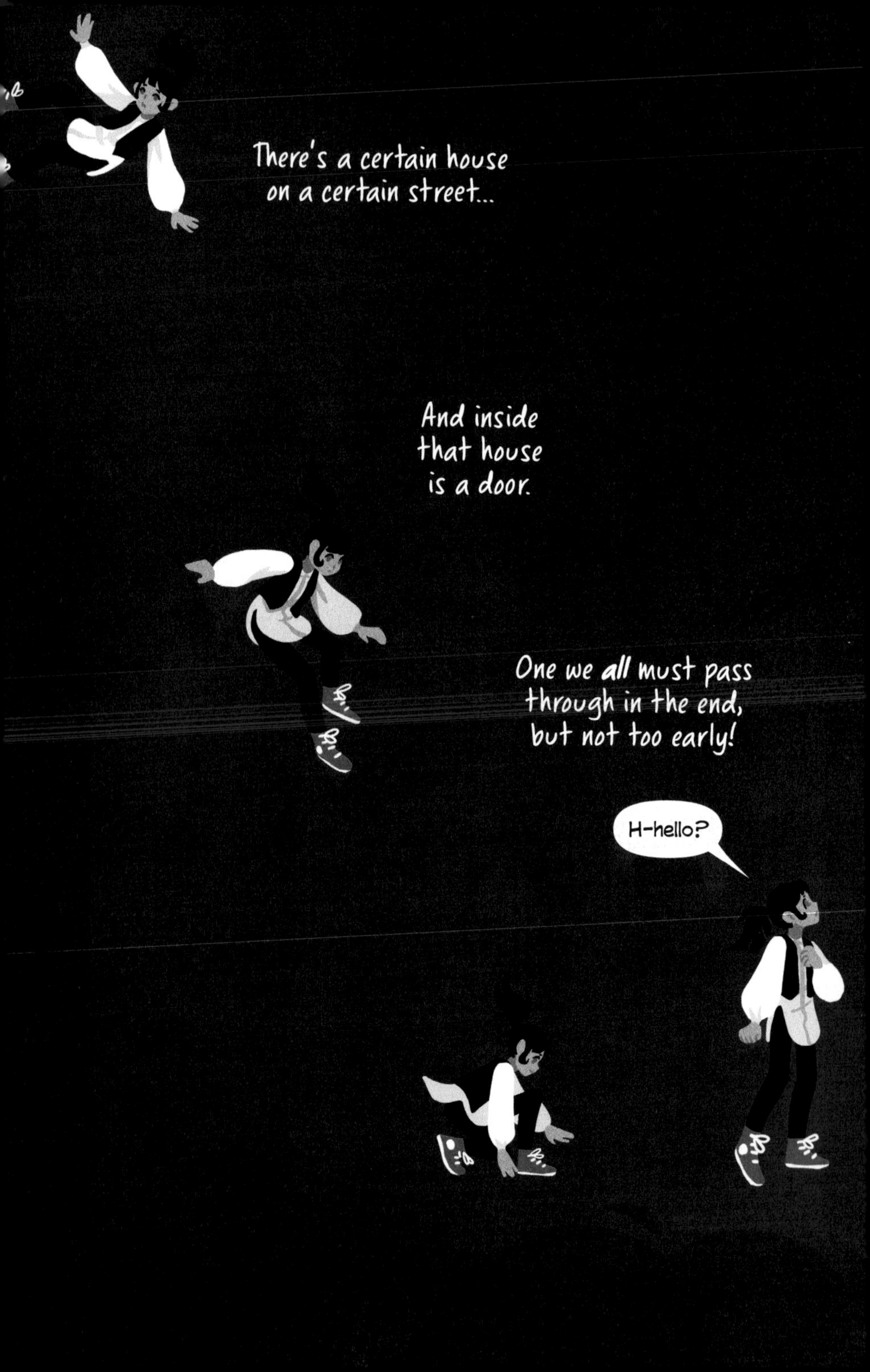
There's a certain house on a certain street...
And inside that house is a door.
One we *all* must pass through in the end, but not too early!
H-hello?

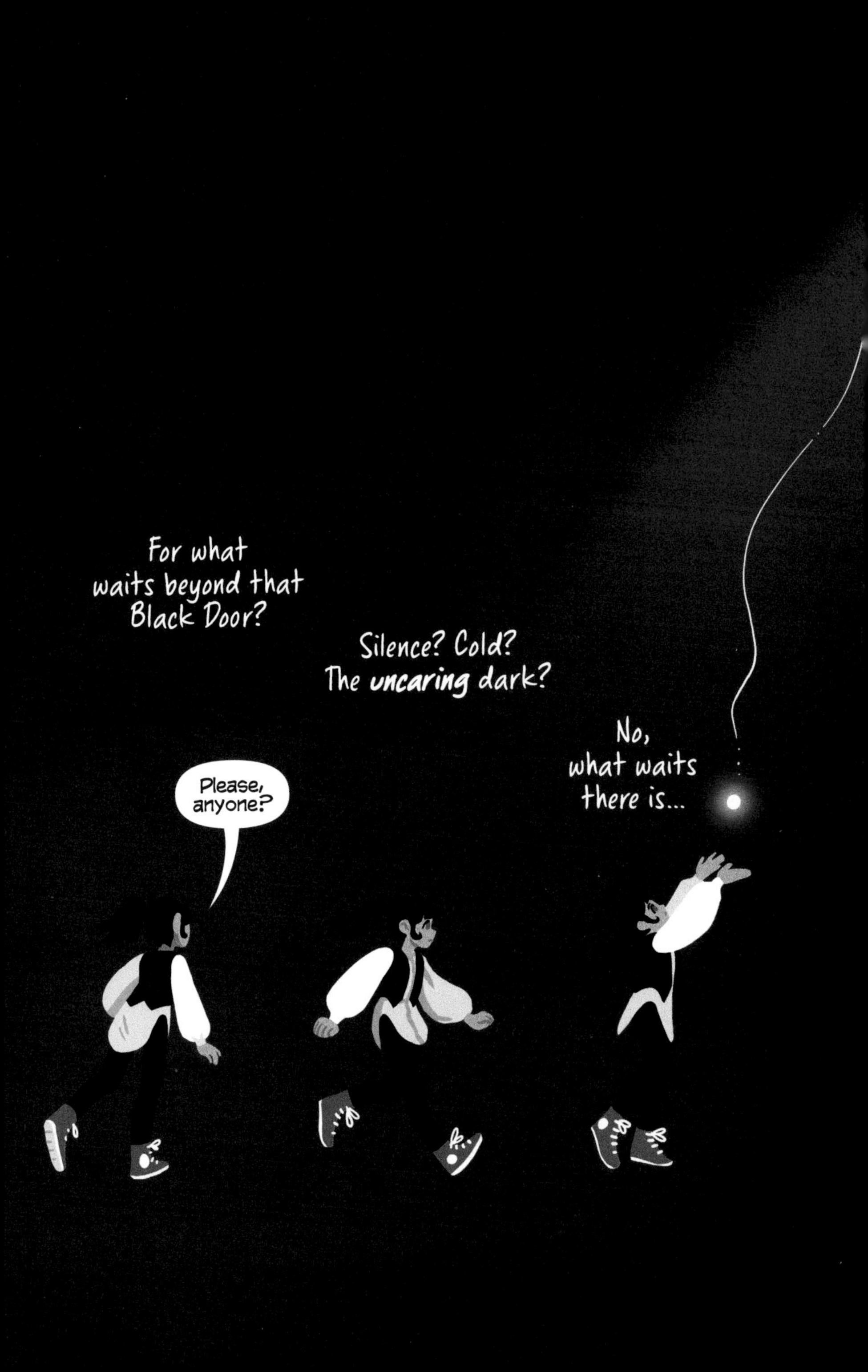

For what
waits beyond that
Black Door?

Silence? Cold?
The *uncaring* dark?

No,
what waits
there is...

Please,
anyone?

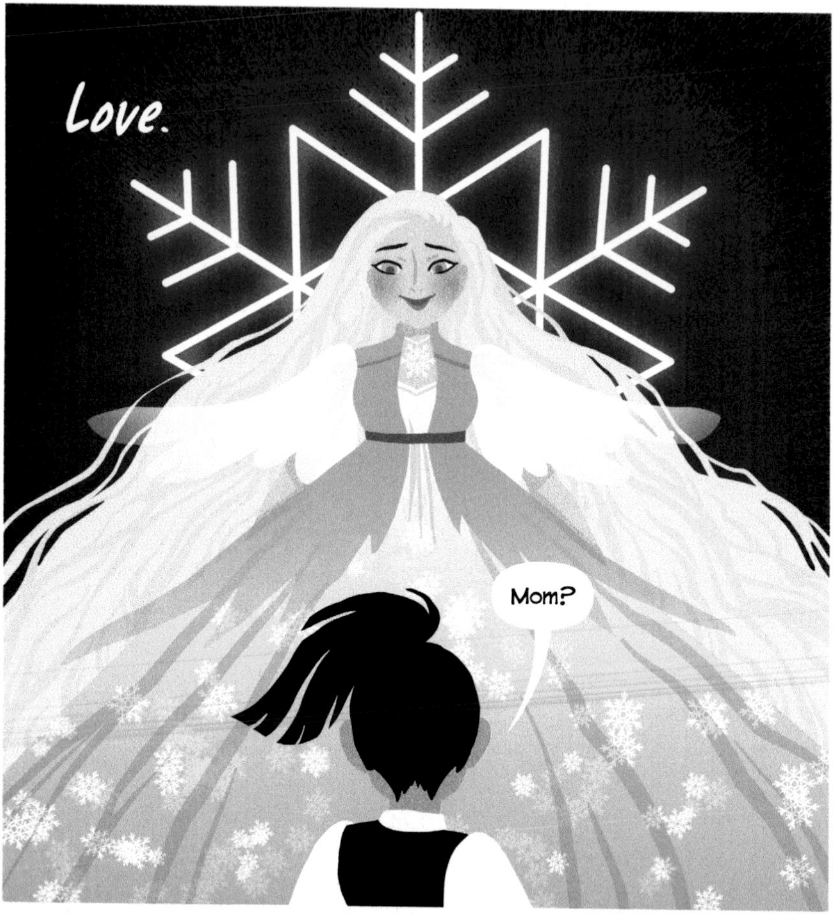
Love.
Mom?

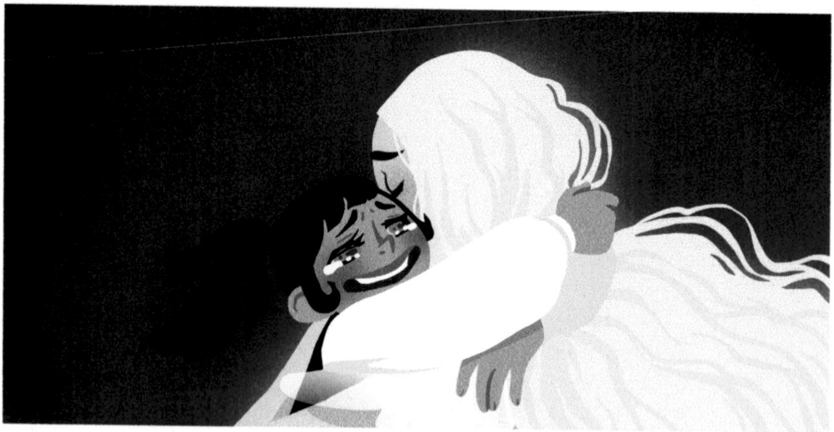

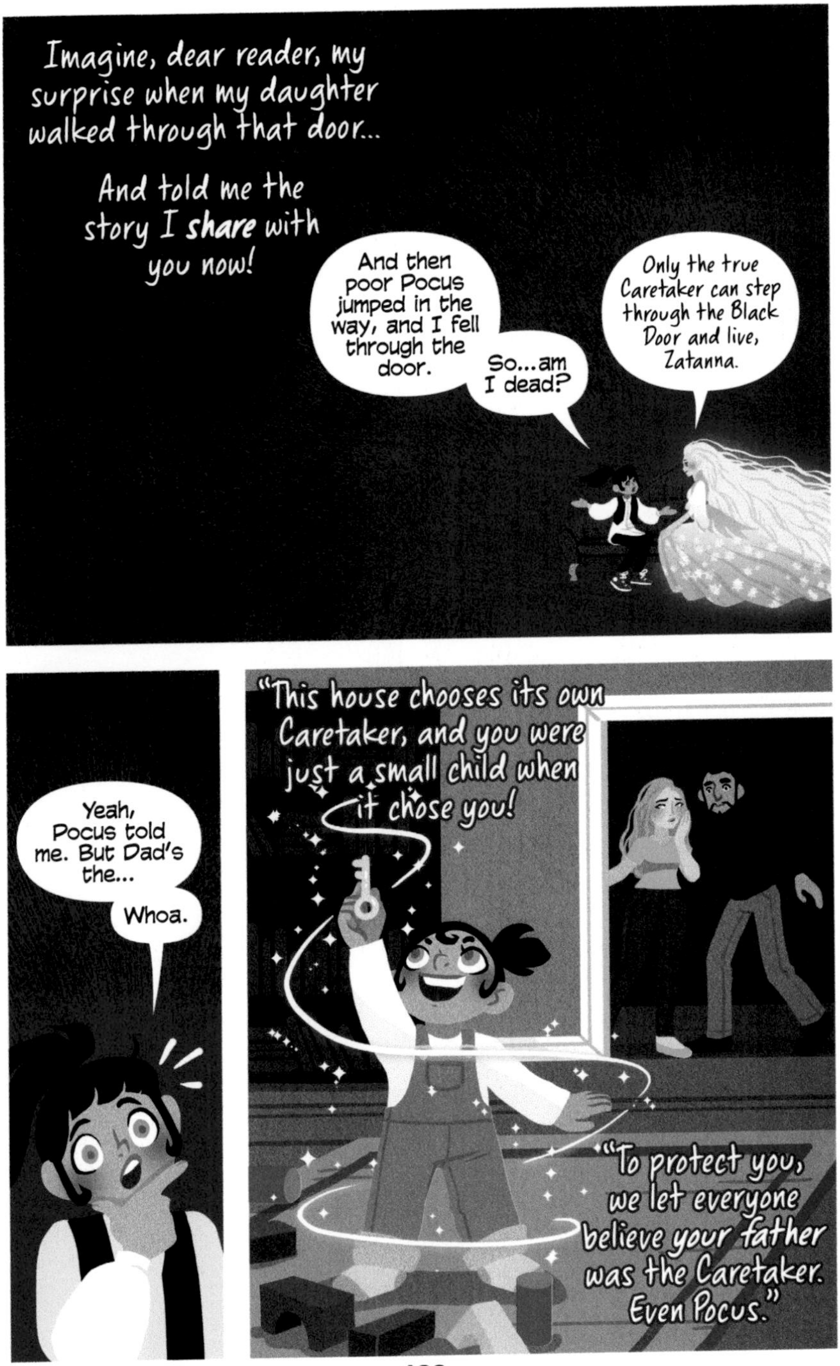

Imagine, dear reader, my surprise when my daughter walked through that door...
And told me the story I **share** with you now!
And then poor Pocus jumped in the way, and I fell through the door.
So...am I dead?
Only the true Caretaker can step through the Black Door and live, Zatanna.
Yeah, Pocus told me. But Dad's the...
Whoa.
"This house chooses its own Caretaker, and you were just a small child when it chose you!
"To protect you, we let everyone believe **your** father was the Caretaker. Even Pocus."

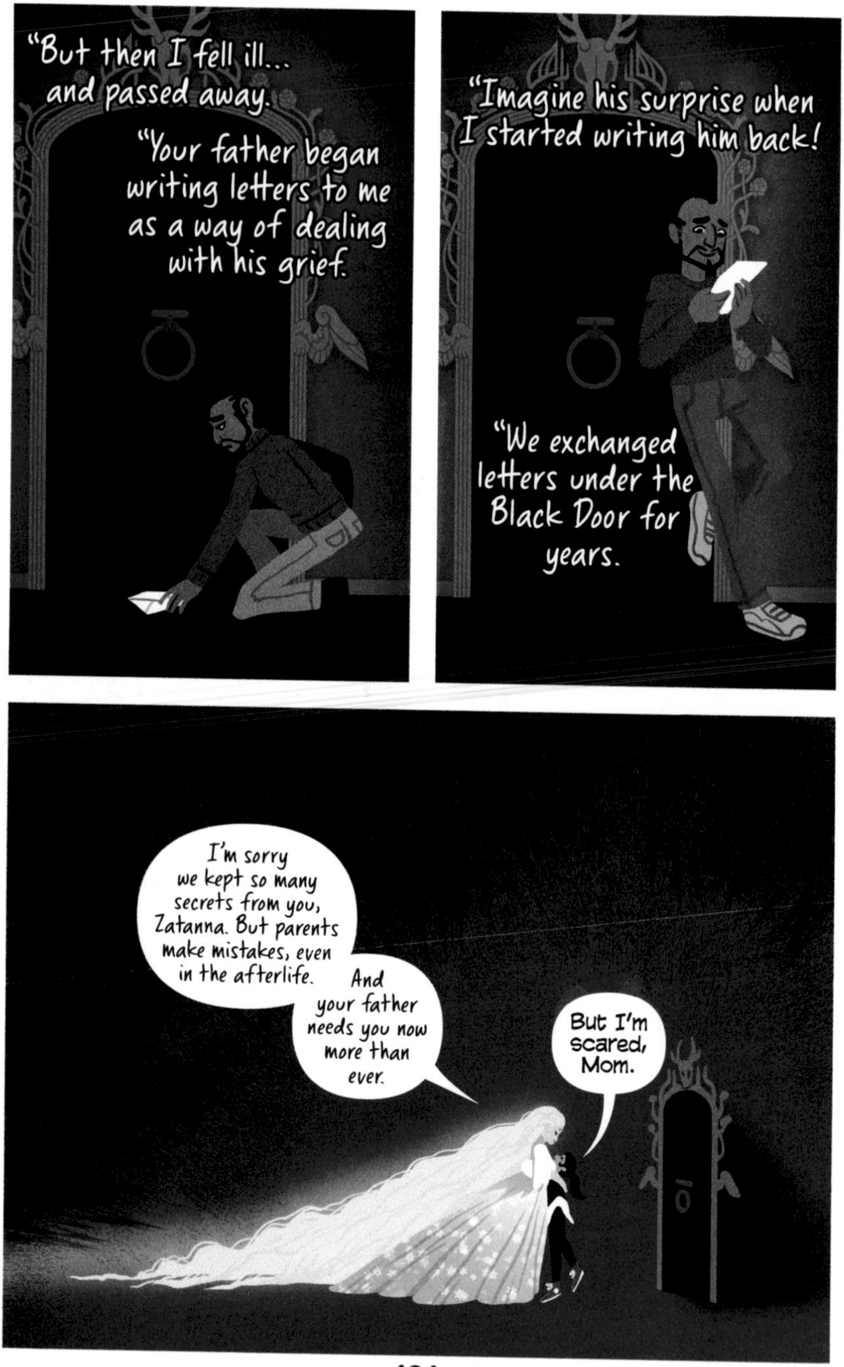
"But then I fell ill... and passed away.
"Your father began writing letters to me as a way of dealing with his grief.
"Imagine his surprise when I started writing him back!
"We exchanged letters under the Black Door for years.
I'm sorry we kept so many secrets from you, Zatanna. But parents make mistakes, even in the afterlife.
And your father needs you now more than ever.
But I'm scared, Mom.

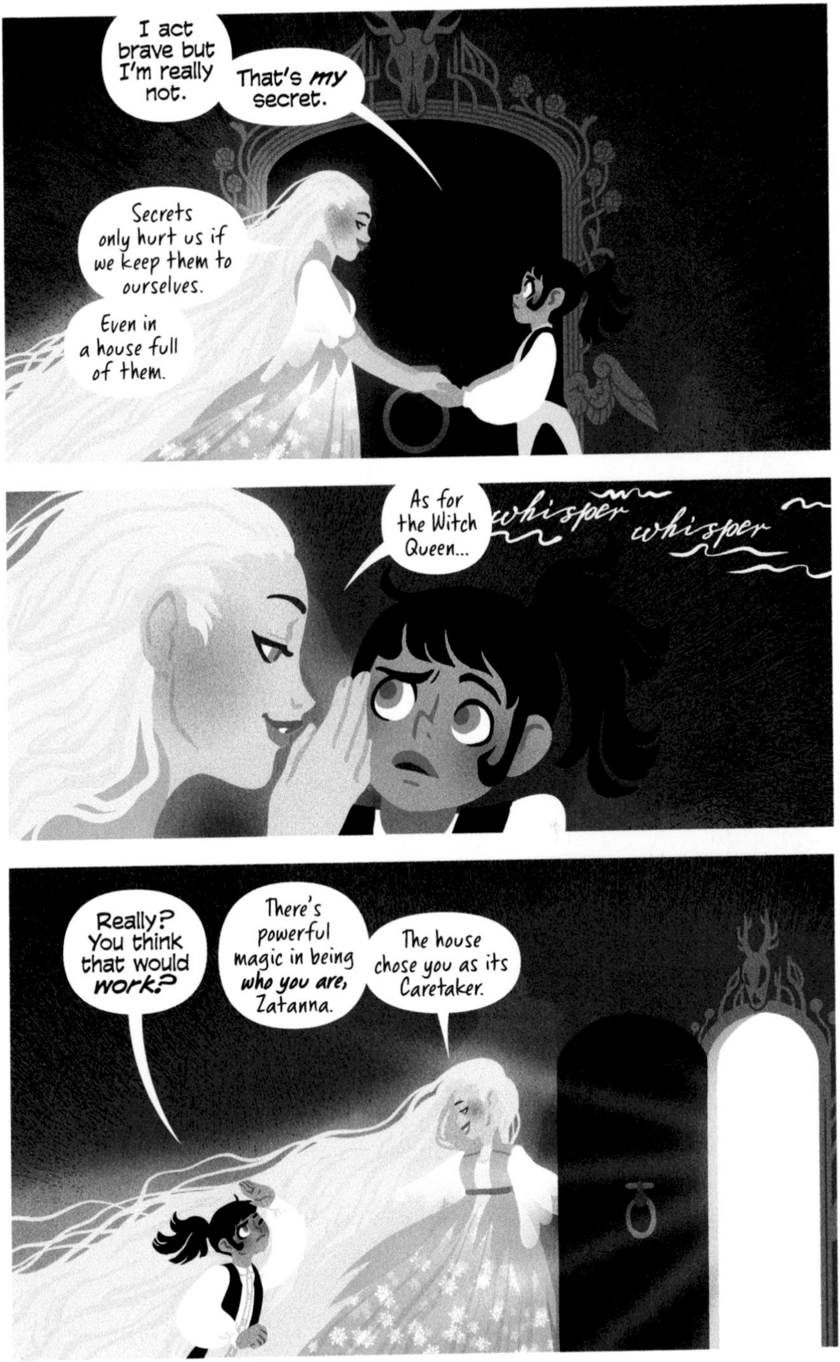
I act brave but I'm really not.
That's *my* secret.
Secrets only hurt us if we keep them to ourselves.
Even in a house full of them.
As for the Witch Queen...
whisper whisper
Really? You think that would *work?*
There's powerful magic in being *who you are*, Zatanna.
The house chose you as its Caretaker.

137

138

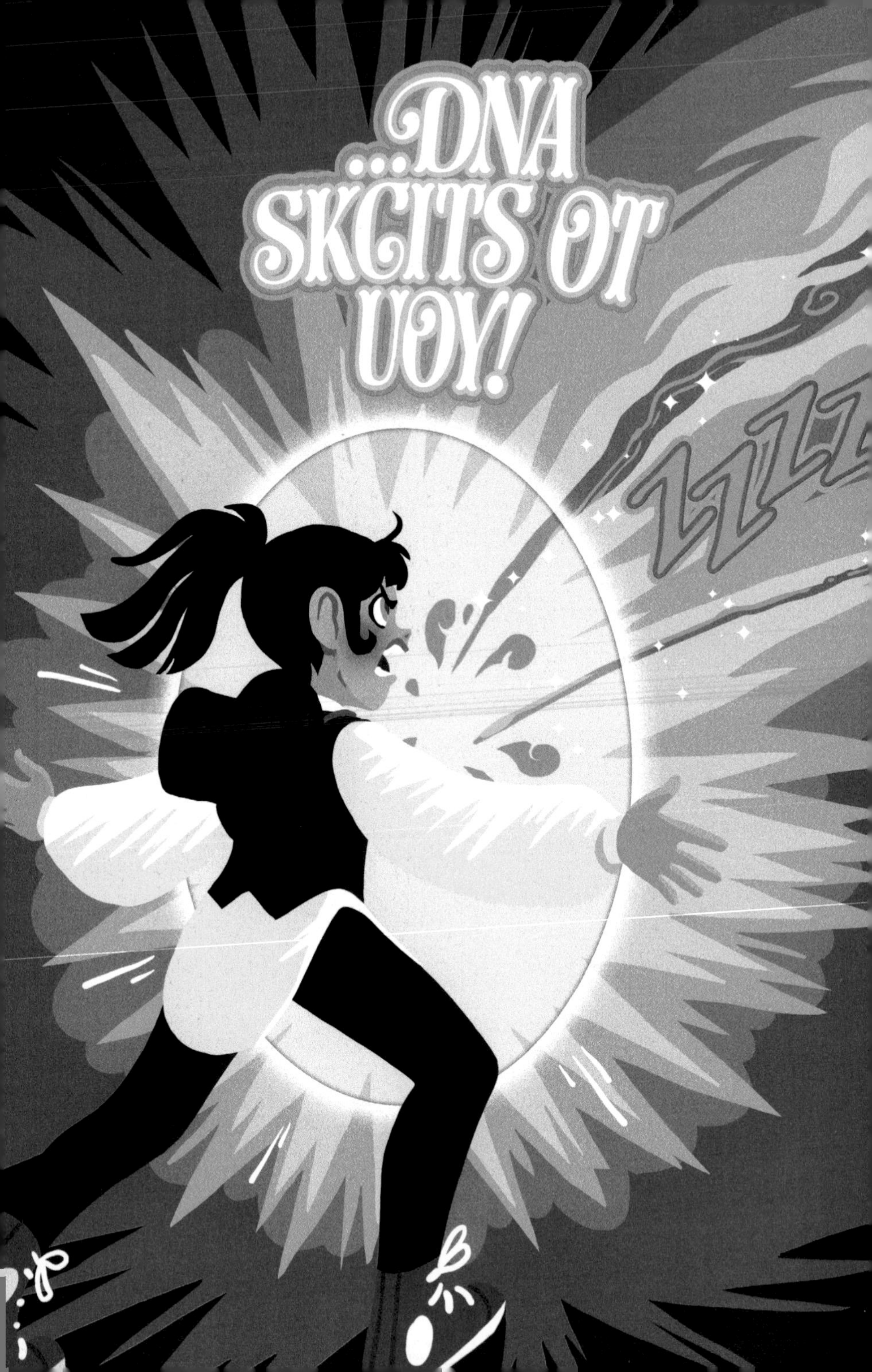
...DNA SKCITS OT UOY!
ZZZ

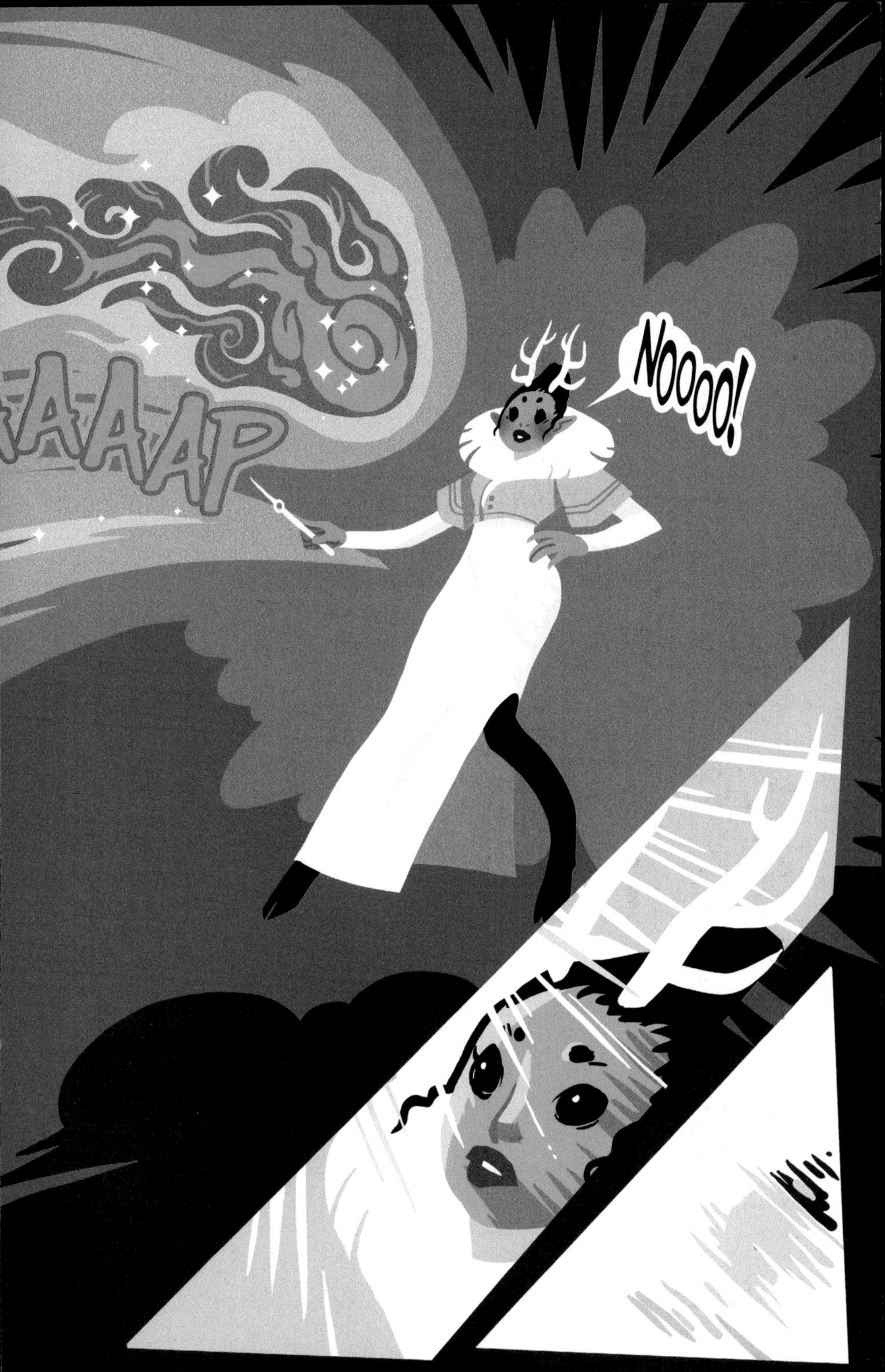
AAAP
NOOOO!

142

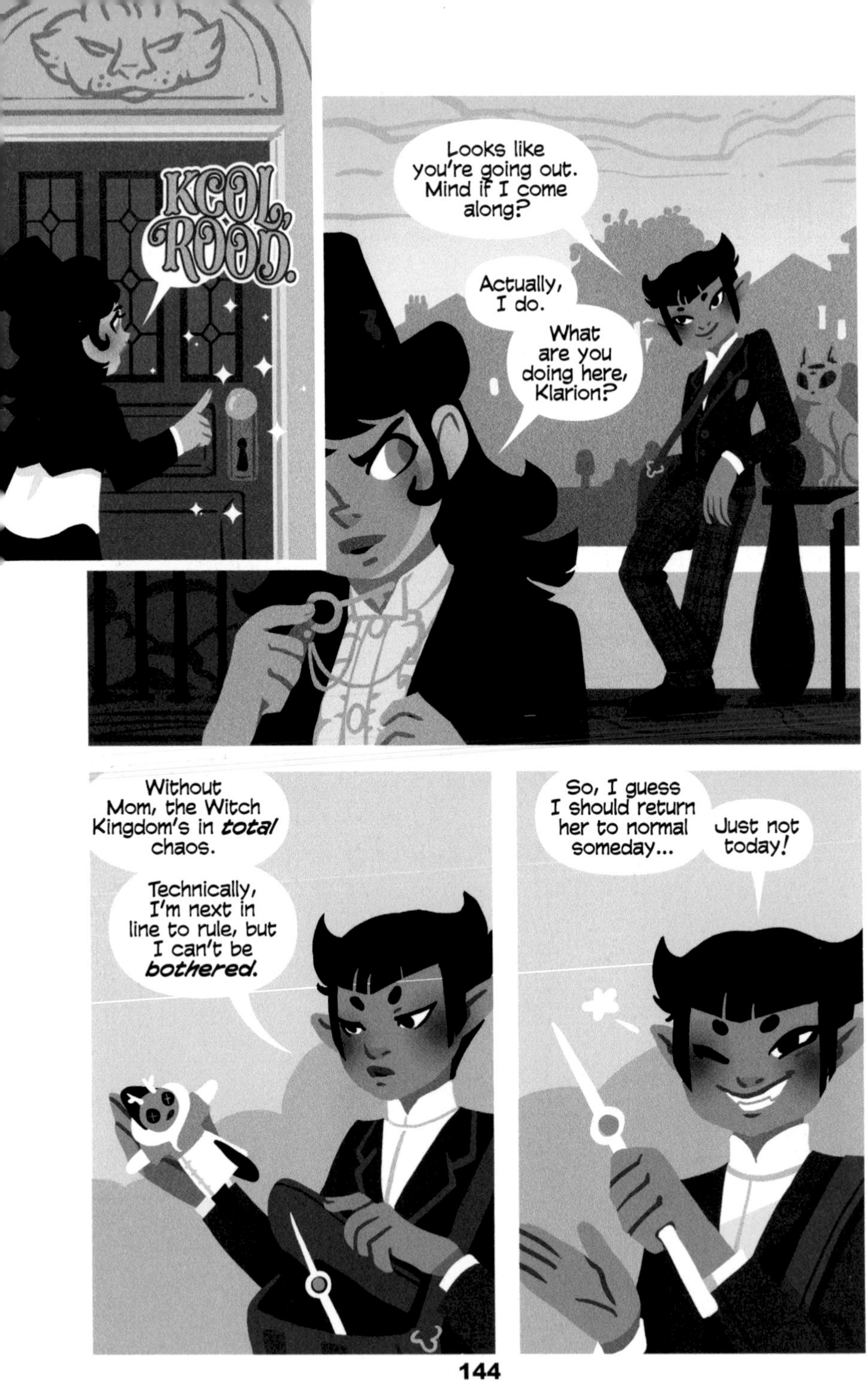
KEOL, ROOD.
Looks like you're going out. Mind if I come along?
Actually, I do.
What are you doing here, Klarion?
Without Mom, the Witch Kingdom's in *total* chaos.
Technically, I'm next in line to rule, but I can't be ***bothered***.
So, I guess I should return her to normal someday...
Just not today!

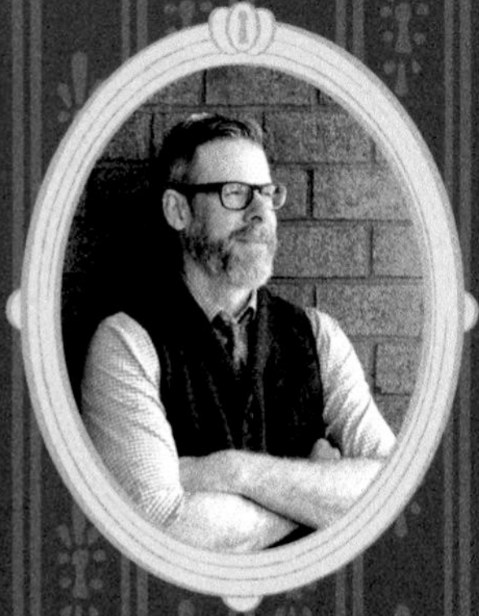

MATTHEW CODY

Matthew Cody is the acclaimed author of several popular children's books including the award-winning Supers of Noble's Green trilogy: *Powerless*, *Super*, and *Villainous*. He lives in Manhattan with his wife and son.

Photo by Alisha McKinney

YOSHI YOSHITANI

Yoshi Yoshitani is a California-based illustrator inspired by fairy tales and bright patterns. Yoshi uses their own multiethnic background to inform their work, creating bold graphic mythologies for the new mixed generation. Originally a concept artist for video games, Yoshi now freelances and creates band posters, book covers, and comics.

IT'S NOT SO EASY BEING A HERO— OR A VILLAIN!

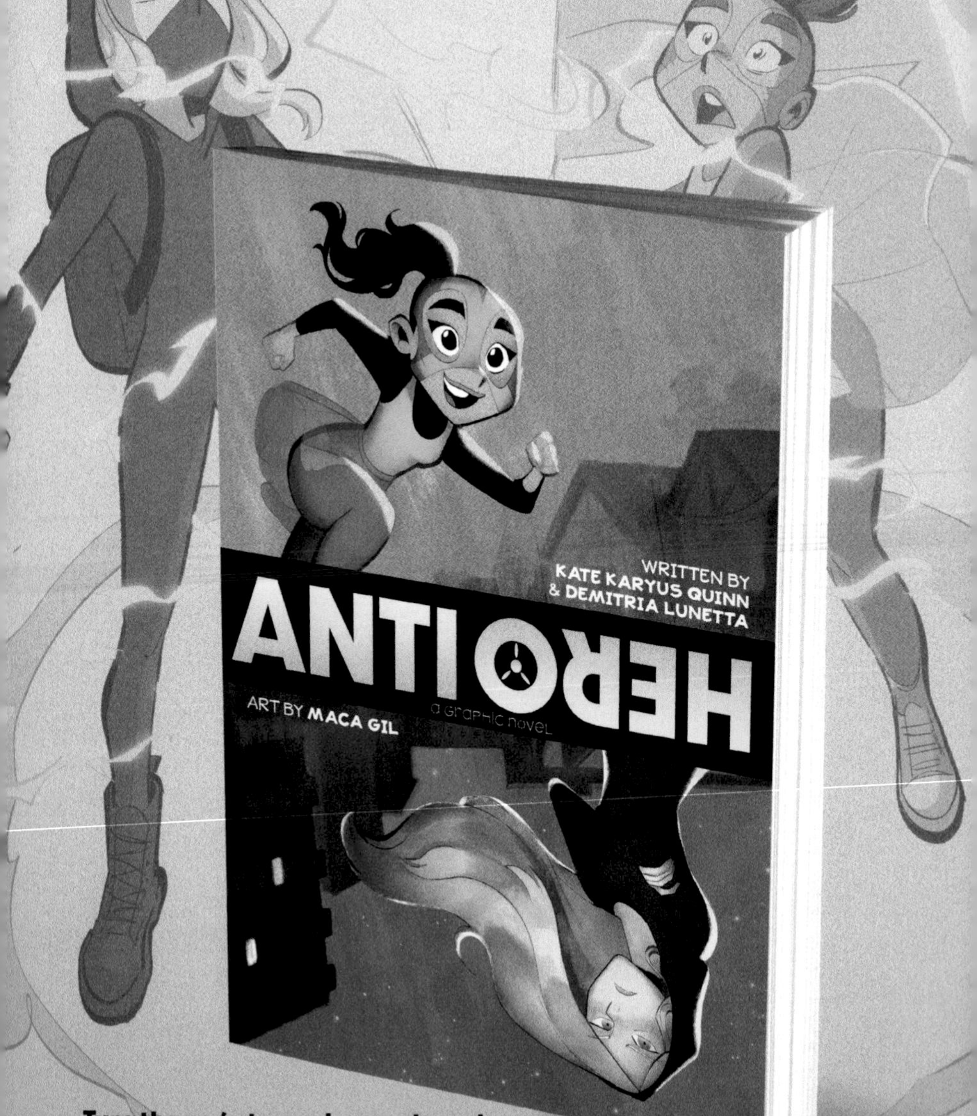

ANTI HERO

a graphic novel

WRITTEN BY KATE KARYUS QUINN & DEMITRIA LUNETTA

ART BY MACA GIL

Turn the page to read a sneak peek of *Anti/Hero*, written by Kate Karyus Quinn and Demitria Lunetta, and illustrated by Maca Gil.

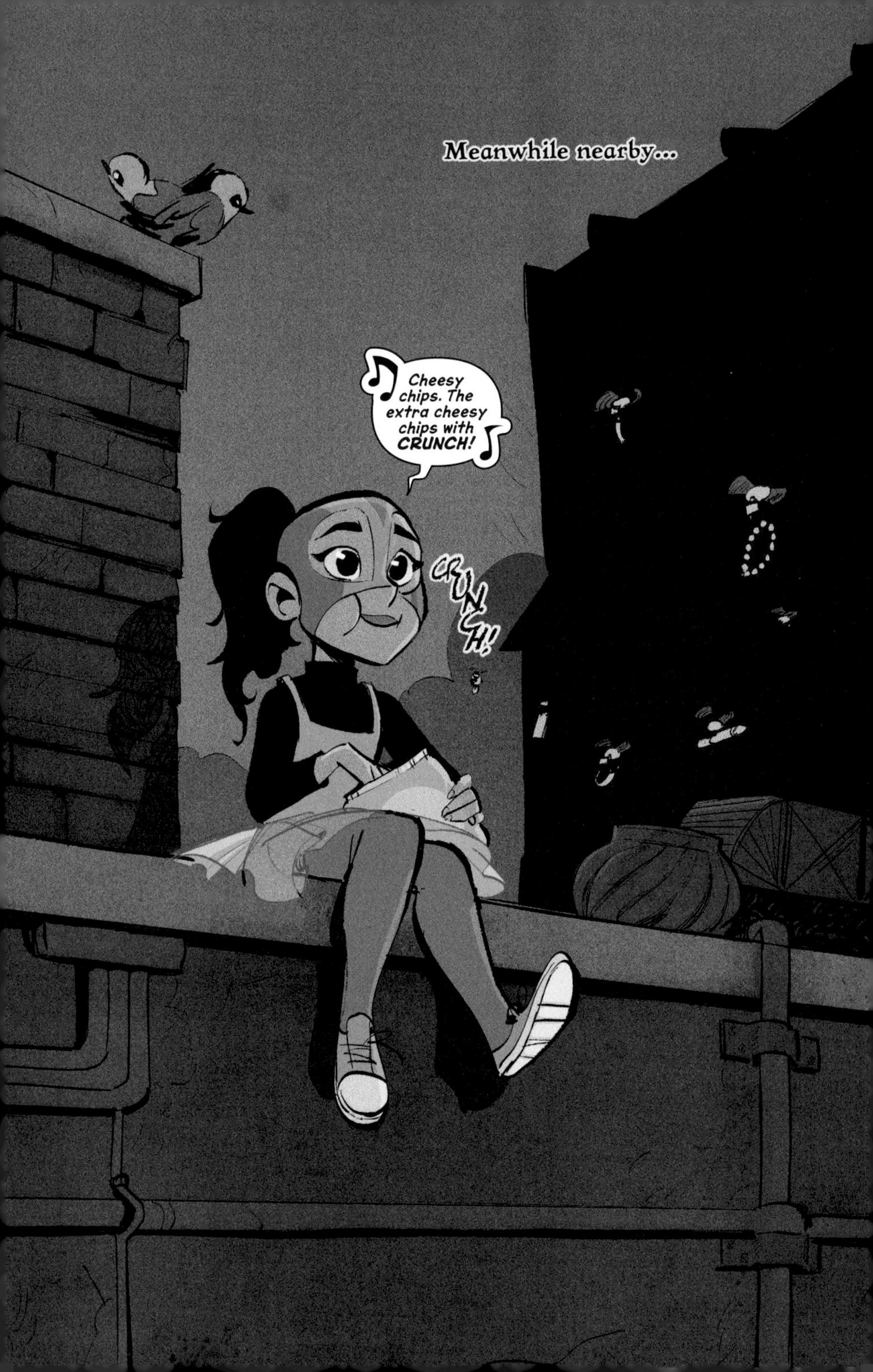

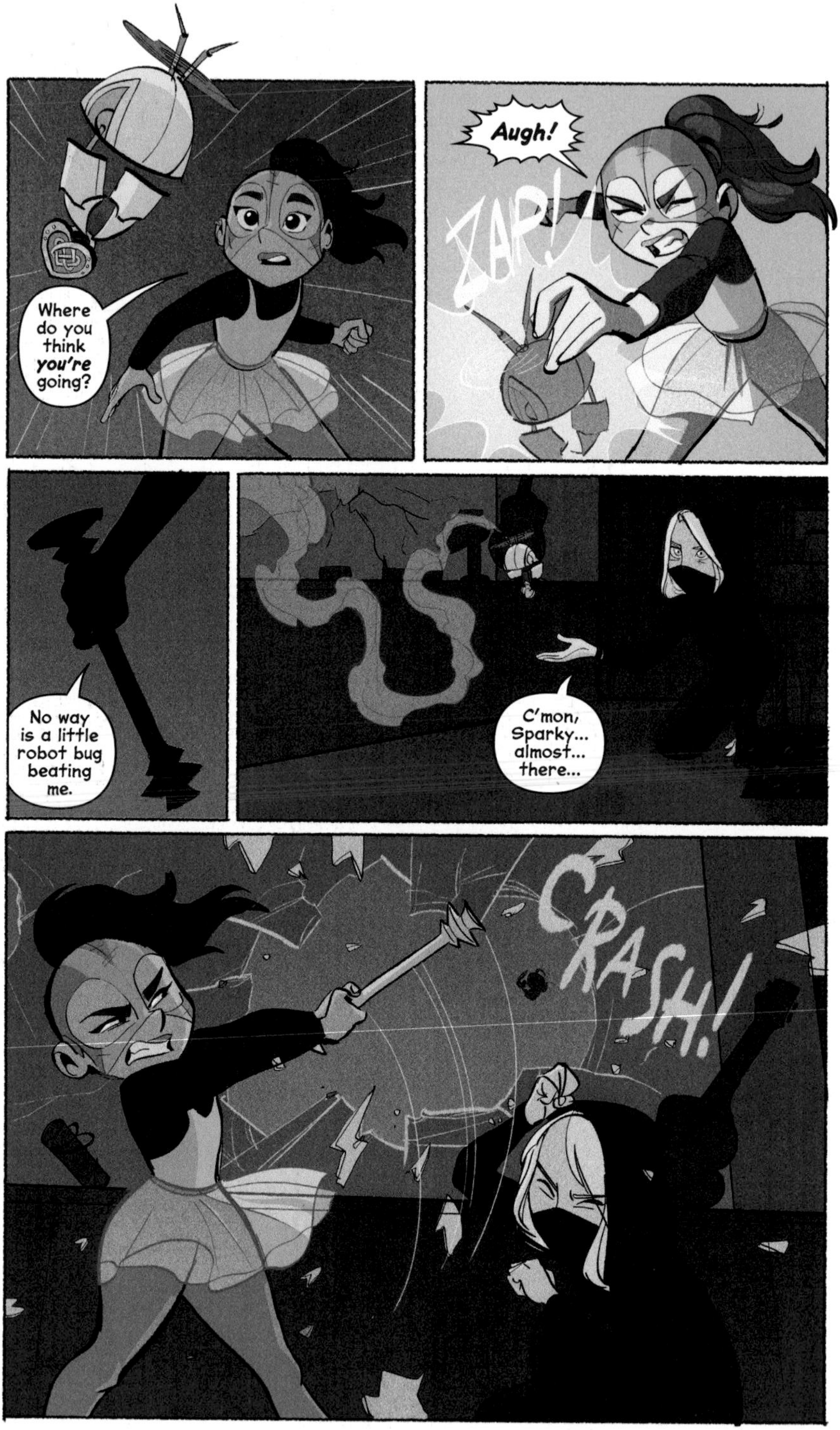
Where do you think *you're* going?
Augh!
ZAP!
No way is a little robot bug beating me.
C'mon, Sparky... almost... there...
CRASH!

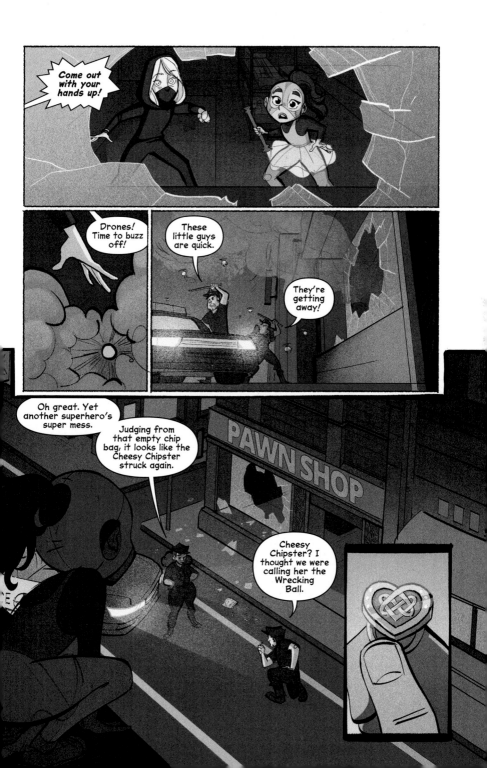

Continues in *Anti/Hero*. On sale April, 2020.

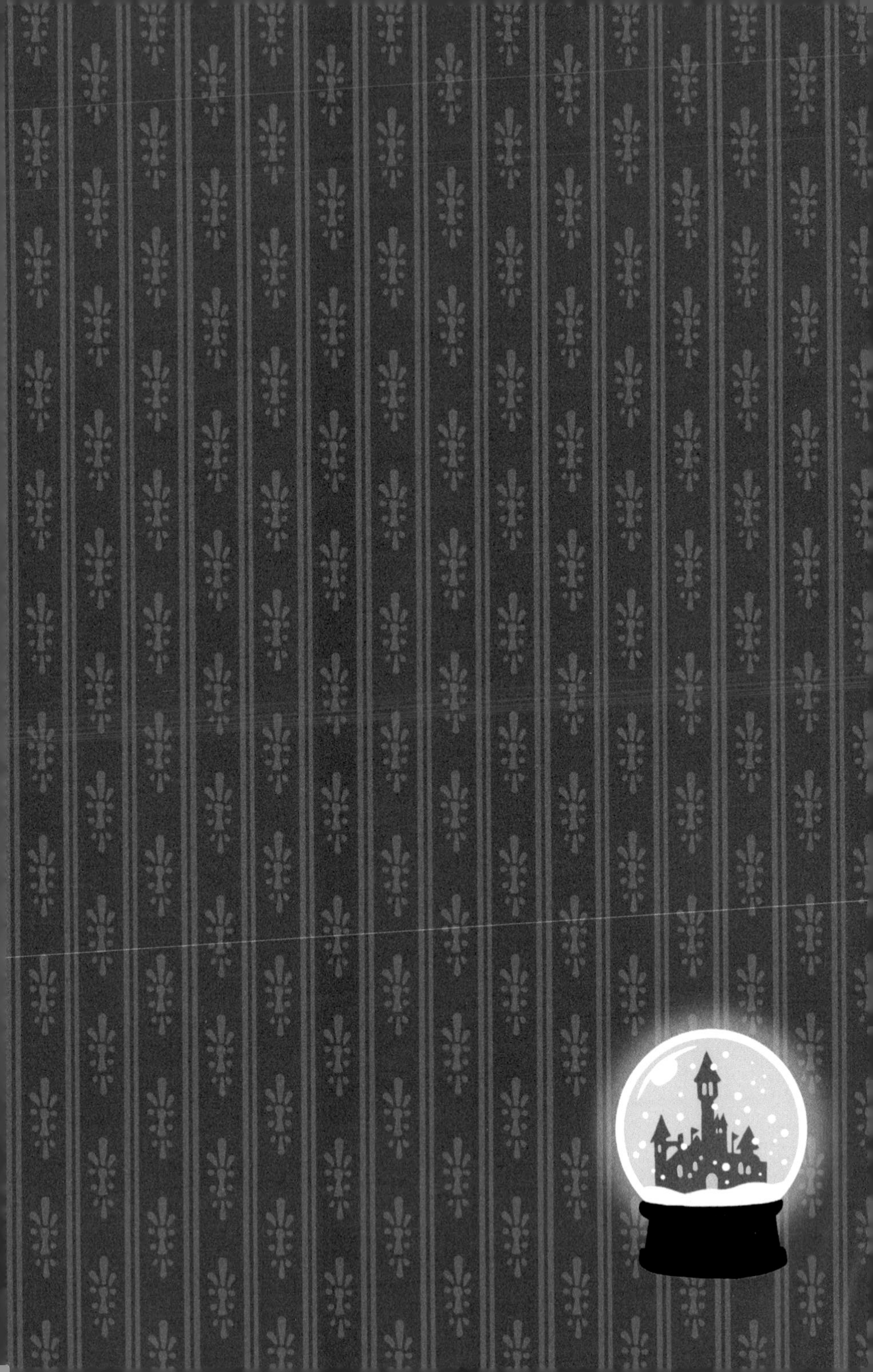